MONOCHROME

SARA J. BERNHARDT

Lavish Publishing LLC

Contents

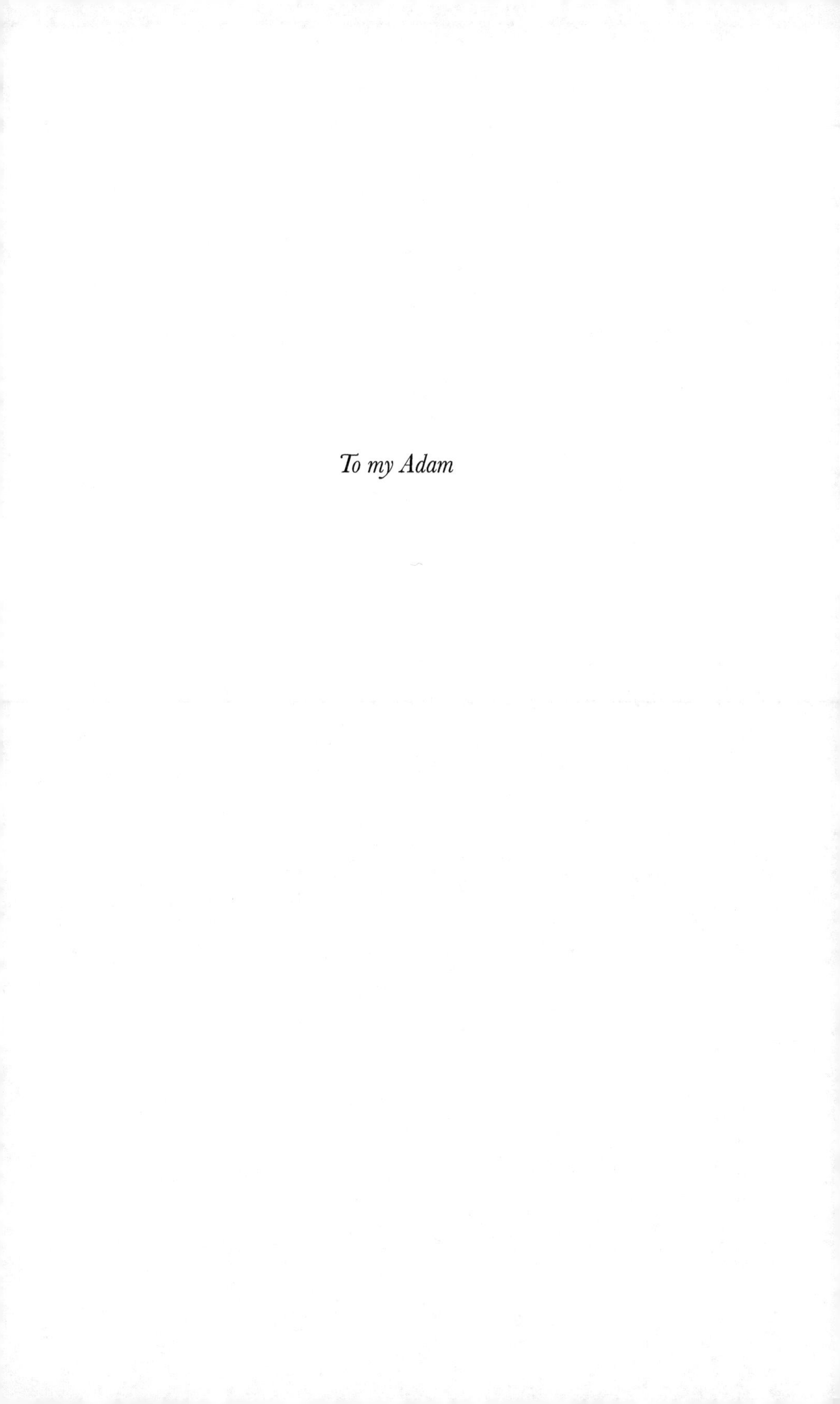

To my Adam

Prologue

I FELT A HOT, stinging pain strike across my back and cried out in agony. My skin burned, and it happened again before I had even a moment to reel from the pain. I heard the loud snap of what had to be a whip.

I didn't bother trying to muffle my screams, it was excruciating. With each blow, I felt wet, warm blood run down my body.

"Please," I begged. "No more."

He struck me again and my entire body shook. I heard the shuffling of feet and hoped it was over; prayed I was alone.

I was still chained to the wall, lurching in pain and simply trying to catch my breath. What a sick bastard. Of course, he wasn't going to kill me right away. He was going to torture me first.

I began to weaken. I had been given no food and no water, and my body was exhausted. I slipped into a light sleep and found myself involuntarily in Daisy's head. I was standing in a field and could see tall grass and trees so high the tops looked like pinpoints. By no choice of mine, I was not in my human form. A breeze ruffled my fur and I saw the girl. Her face was sullen and blank. Her eyes were rimmed with tears.

"Oh, Daisy, please don't be sad for me," I cooed, trying to express my compassion.

"Lucas?" She turned around, searching for me. She was so beautiful, and I hated seeing her looking so lost.

"Down here," I responded.

She peered down and met my eyes. "Oh, Lucas. I miss you."

"I know. Please don't be sad." It was hard to look at her; hard to see what I had caused. Her face was ashen, and her gaze was confused and far away.

Soft tears slid down her cheeks. "Why did you leave me?"

I inhaled, trying to get a hold of myself. "I had to."

She sighed slowly, shaking her head. "Why?"

My own pain was almost unbearable. I couldn't stand inflicting it on Daisy. My chest burned but I tried to stay composed for her sake.

"Daisy, I always have a reason for the things I do, even if you don't understand them. I love you. I had to save you. Someone had to pay for my mistakes; the only person who should be punished is me."

I was pulled from the dream by a splash of water on my face. I shook my head, trying to shed the fogginess from my eyes. My vision cleared, and I saw Moe standing in front of me.

"Oh, Lucas," he murmured.

"Moe—please."

"I shouldn't really be here," he murmured, "but I convinced them to let me see you. I brought you some water."

My mouth was dry, and my lips were parched and cracked.

I almost felt ravenous at the thought of water. He brought a small cup to my lips and I drank hungrily. He pulled away.

"More please," I begged.

He lifted the cup again and as he pulled away, I leaned forward, trying to get more.

"Lucas, you can't have too much. It's going to go right through you."

I hadn't even thought of that. At the time, I didn't care. I felt as if it were impossible to drink enough to quench my thirst.

"I need more," I groaned, "please."

He pursed his lips for a moment but let me drink a bit more from the cup. The coolness coursed through my body, relieving some of the discomfort.

"I'll come back when I can with something for you to eat. Don't say anything to them about it."

"Why would I say anything to those pigs?"

"You need to keep your mouth in check too, boy. It will be worse for you if you don't."

I didn't respond. He disappeared in the dark and, for the first time, I found myself wishing he would stay.

I tried to sooth some of the pain in my shoulders but shifting didn't help. The cuffs were iron and left little room to move. I groaned and whimpered at the persistent, unwavering misery. I just wanted them to kill me. I couldn't stay here like this, just waiting for them to come back and hurt me again.

I was slipping into unconsciousness when the sound of footsteps alerted me. I braced myself and felt that same hot pain across the length of my entire back. I could feel the warmth of my own blood and see it dripping to the floor. Mr. White moved from behind me and looked into my tired eyes. He didn't say a word and struck me hard across my face. I groaned, and he hit me again and again until I tasted my own blood in my mouth. He hit me over and over until I lost half my vision. My left eye had swollen shut.

"You'll show me a bit more respect," he growled, "or I will draw this out even longer."

The recent beating had me wishing once again that he would just get it over with and kill me!

I cannot say how many more days I was there. Moe was right about having too much water. I tried with every ounce of will power I had to avoid letting my body give in, but it was to no avail and I was soiled myself. I felt sick and disgusted at how pathetic I was. I had never been so helpless in my life.

Moe came back a few times with some water and bits of food, only enough to keep me alive. All my muscles were strained, tense and aching horribly. My body was frail, and my mind was cloudy.

I watched Moe approach me.

"Oh, god, Lucas," he said. "Did he do this to you?"

"You know he did," I choked out.

"Oh, Son…"

"What is it?"

He made a sound and leaned in closer to see. "Brace yourself."

"Why?"

"Your jaw is dislocated."

"Yeah, it feels that way."

He raised his hand but hesitated a moment. He grasped under my chin and pulled with an agonizing crack. I cried out briefly but a wave of relief came over me.

"Thanks. I need you to do one more thing for me."

He scoffed. "What do you expect me to do?"

"Kill me," I groaned, "please."

"Do you actually expect me to do that?"

"I'm asking you to," I moaned on the verge of tears. "Please."

"Don't be ridiculous, Lucas. I'm taking you home."

All my thoughts halted and, for a brief moment, I forgot about the pain in my body. "What?"

"I begged them for leniency. You've been through enough."

I sighed, feeling immensely relieved. Maybe I would get to see Daisy one last time. When he released me from the cuffs, the pain in my arms and shoulders was almost immobilizing. He helped me to my feet and took me to the car. I slumped in my seat, barely able to stay conscious. Moe didn't say a word as he drove, but I could feel both his anger over what had happened and his empathy for me. It was the first time I really felt he loved me.

After arriving at his place, he basically carried me into the house.

"I need to get you cleaned up," he said.

He helped me roll over onto my stomach and ripped off what was left of my shirt. He blotted at the lashes on my back with an alcohol-soaked cloth. It stung horribly and I winced, involuntarily groaning.

"Oh stop," Moe huffed, "It's not that bad."

I scoffed.

"Trust me, Son, I've seen worse."

"Then why are you still there, Moe? Why do you still associate yourself with that organization? It's evil."

"Lucas, let's not do this, all right? I just want to get you better first."

My bones were broken and my skin was cut, burned, and bruised. There wasn't much he could do for my broken ribs except wrap me up. He left me for a short while to sleep and woke me later to help me into the bath. He took off the wraps and helped me stumble into the bathroom.

"I'm going to give you some privacy" he said, "but I'm right outside if you need me."

After my mom left, Moe just sort of shut down. He had never been as much a father to me as he was in the moments he took care of me. It touched me deeply.

"Thank you, Moe," I said, "Really. For everything."

He nodded but remained silent, unsure how to respond.

I soaked in the tub enjoying the softness of water on my sore skin and enjoying the heat soothing my tense muscles. I forced myself to stand up and rinse off so I wasn't just sitting in filthy water. It wasn't easy staying on my feet, but I was able to just long enough.

Moe put the wraps back on and gave me some new clothes to wear.

"I made you a plate," he said.

"Thanks."

"Sure."

"Moe, where is…"

"She's fine," he said, raising his hands. "Look—there was something we had to do."

I sighed. "I really don't like the sound of that."

"Lucas, things are a real mess right now because of this girl. The best we can do is make her forget."

I felt a sort of ache come into my chest. "What?"

"It's the only way for things to go back to normal."

"Moe—that won't work."

"What are you talking about? Of course, it will work."

"No," I retorted, "It won't. Daisy remembers me. She remembers everything."

"Even so, if nobody else does they can just as easily convince her she was dreaming."

I shook my head, "Is there no other way?"

He shook his head. "I'm sorry, Son."

I couldn't stand the thought of her forgetting me all over again. I had made her fall in love with me so many times before and now that I finally had her, I was forced to lose her. My grief was unbearable. I promised her she would never forget me; that things between us would be fine. I hated myself for breaking the most important promise I ever made to her.

____

Chapter 1

____

THE AIR WAS crisp and cool, biting through my sweatshirt. Anxiety set in, and I would never forgive myself if I didn't get there in time. I quickened my pace until I came to the little blue house on the corner. My memory flashed with haunting images of what I knew would happen if I did nothing. I watched impatiently, wanting more than anything to react but knowing I had to be patient. Timing was everything.

The ball rolled into the street and my body twitched, ready to jump into action. The familiar little boy I saw in my dream reached the end of his driveway, in pursuit of the toy. I sprang into action, racing toward the middle of the street, my body lagged behind my legs, but I pushed myself as hard as I could. I leaned forward and scooped the boy into my arms. I felt a gust of wind at my back as the truck sped by, inches from turning us into a bloody puddle in the middle of the road. The horn blared in my ears as I ran. I set the boy down in the grass of his yard.

"Stay out of the street," I said.

His eyes were wide and rimmed with tears. He gave me a feeble nod which was enough for me. He was traumatized enough to have learned his lesson.

I sighed heavily, catching my breath. I ran my hands through my tangled hair and headed back toward home. I thought I heard the kid call out to me, but I ignored it. The less contact I had with anyone, the better.

"Hey, where were you?" Jess asked, tucking her phone into her back pocket. "I was just about to call you."

"I didn't have my phone," I said. "I didn't want to worry you and I really had to take care of something."

"You had a dream, didn't you?"

I nodded. "I woke up with that—pull. I knew it was today."

"And?"

"I'm fine. The kid's fine too."

"A kid?" she bellowed.

"Yeah, a little boy. He chased a ball into the street, but he's okay."

She shook her head, sighing to herself. "They stopped for a while, didn't they?"

"Yeah, but they always come back—eventually."

"Any more flashbacks?"

I shook my head. "I have nightmares sometimes, but I haven't dreamed of the crash since I met Lucas." His name caught in my throat. I knew Jess picked up on it, but she didn't mention it.

"Let's do something fun," she said, with false cheer in her voice.

I raised my eyebrows. "Like what?"

She pursed her lips, and looked away, "Umm…how about…" she broke off.

"There's nothing to do here," I bantered, smirking.

She shrugged. "Well, we have the whole house to ourselves."

"Yeah, and?"

"And…" she sighed and reached under her bed. "I got this a while ago but wasn't sure it was the right time to bring it up."

She pulled out a big bottle of red wine.

I laughed. "Jess, do you remember what happened the last time we did this?"

She smiled. "It came out of the carpet—eventually."

I laughed. "How did you even get this?"

"Curtis," she said, as if it was obvious.

"Your brother buys you wine?"

She shrugged, "He's pretty cool most the time."

"He's not going to be here, right?"

She shook her head. "No, he's back at the university already. He won't be back again until Thanksgiving—or maybe Christmas."

"You still have that corkscrew?" I asked.

"Somewhere," she answered, "but—I couldn't find it last time I looked."

I scoffed, "Well that's great. We can't open the bottle without it."

"Nonsense," she sang. "Where's that Daisy Carmichael creativity?" she eyed me playfully.

I smiled, "Fine," I rolled my eyes, "gimmie your shoe."

"My what?"

I waved my hand at her. "You heard me, come on."

She gave me an odd look but took off her sneaker and handed it to me. "Whatever you say. Crazy."

I mock glared at her and placed the wine between my knees to stabilize it. I started pounding at the cork with the sole of her shoe.

She started laughing. "If your crazy ass breaks the bottle, my mom will kill the both of us."

"I'm not going to break it."

I continued hitting the cork until it plunked into the bottle.

"Ha!" I yelled. "See?"

She shook her head and peered at the cork bobbing in the wine. "Whatever works," she said, laughing.

We grabbed a couple of plastic wine glasses we bought at the dollar store a couple years ago.

"So," Jess started, raising her glass, "what should we toast to?"

"To friendship."

"Sure, cheese ball," she snickered.

"Well, what do *you* want to toast to?"

She smirked at me. "How about to still being able to have fun in spite of everything."

"To wine, then."

She laughed. "To wine." She tapped her glass against mine.

"This *is* fun," I said.

She nodded, taking a sip from her glass. "Oh, I almost forgot to tell you. I think I've decided what I want to major in."

"What do you mean?" I asked. "I thought you decided to go with child development."

She shook her head. "It didn't feel right," she said, thoughtfully. "I'm thinking art."

I grinned widely. "Seriously?"

"Yeah," she tilted her head, "why are you so surprised?"

"It's not that, it's just—did I have anything to do with that?"

"Maybe a little. You've always loved art. I guess you inspired me a bit."

"Your parents are going to lose it."

"I know," she sighed. "They want me to be a doctor. Or a lawyer, like Curt."

I shook my head, smiling. "You always were the black sheep. Hey, maybe we can take some classes together. Although, I need to find something else to major in now."

"What?" she almost shouted. "Daisy, art has always been your—dream. You can't give up on it."

"Jess, I haven't painted since the accident. Colors…"

"I understand," she interrupted and then paused before continuing, "but don't you want to try again someday?"

I shook my head. "Art is still who I am, but I'm thinking about getting more into something like photography. That's still artistic. And I did talk to my mom once about journalism."

She shrugged. "Do whatever you want. I just don't want you to lose yourself because of what's happened to you."

I smiled. "I know, and I love you for that, Jess. I'm the same crazy person I've always been."

She smiled back and raised her glass again. "To being crazy."

Chapter 2

I STRETCHED *out my stiff fingers and closed my notebook. Switching off the lamp on my desk, I thought about heading to bed early in hopes that, by morning, the thoughts I was having would be gone. At least for a while. It only took seconds to realize there was no way I would be able to sleep. I crept down the hall and hesitantly reached for the handle of the door.*

I knocked lightly on the door, deciding not to intrude. "Mom?"

"It's open." I blew out a breath at the muffled response.

I peeked inside. She was wearing her pink nightgown, the one I gave her for her birthday a couple of years before. She looked up from the book she was reading and took off her reading glasses. "You okay?"

She always knew when something was wrong. I shrugged. "I don't know."

She signaled me with her hand. "Come here."

I crawled into bed beside her like I did when I was little.

"What's going on?" She stared at me so solidly, waiting for me to come clean. "There's nothing you can't tell me."

I sighed, looking for the words. "I've just been thinking."

"About?"

"Nothing," I deflected, "it's not important."

"Daisy, it's okay. Whatever it is."

*"You don't talk about it." I groused, bordering on desperation. "You **won't** talk about it."*

She sighed. "This is about your dad, isn't it?"

I looked away, almost afraid to see the look in her eyes. I nodded.

"I'm sorry," she murmured. "I know it's not fair to you. I should have told you more about your father. It's just... It's hard for me, Daisy."

"It's hard for me, too. I don't even remember him. At least you know who he was."

"I know. I never should have kept this from you. I guess I should have realized what it meant to you. I think I'm ready to answer some questions you might have."

"I just want to know..."

"Know what?"

"Everything. What he was like."

She reached over and took my hands in hers. "Well, he was sweet; charming. He had an idealistic view of the world, a little like you. He believed in magic and happily ever after. I see him in you sometimes."

"Really?"

"The way you paint and the words you write. You see the world through the same rose-colored glasses. It's something I loved about him and I love that you have that same quality. He was always upbeat, making jokes. Even after a rough day, he found a way to smile. He made the house such a warm place."

"I wish I could remember."

She looked away for a moment. "He loved you, Daisy. More than anything."

"I know. I just feel an emptiness sometimes, like something is missing."

"So do I, but you still got me. That's something, right?" She smiled.

I giggled. "Yeah, You're all right."

She smacked my arm. "Brat."

I stuck my tongue out at her.

She put her arm around me and pulled me close. "Let's watch a movie."

"Now?" I realized we were done talking about Dad. At least for now.

"I'm not tired, are you?"

"Well, no, but you usually make me go to bed around now. It's a school night."

She winked. "I won't tell if you don't."

I smiled. "Okay, sure." She even let me eat popcorn in bed, unconcerned about the mess. She let me fall asleep next to her like I was still a little girl.

Time with my mom was always comforting. Any confusion, or teenage angst, or fear of the future was completely forgotten. With Mom, I knew everything would be okay. No matter what.

Chapter 3

DEAREST DAISY,

Since Kristoff's initiation and acceptance into The Order, things have felt a bit different. There are many things he is not permitted to tell me, things I feel he should want to talk about.

It doesn't make sense that, after everything, he still wants to be a part of it. I might have understood associating with them, but to join an organization responsible for the torture and near death of his own flesh and blood feels like a betrayal. I guess I just have to accept that Kristoff will do what he feels is right, whether I agree with him or not. I'll see you as soon as I can. I love you.

Lucas.

I sighed, folding the letter into the worn-down creases, and tucked it back into my desk drawer for the third time that day.

"Hey, you okay?" Jess asked, scattering my thoughts.

"Um, yeah. Just thinking."

"Were you reading that letter again?"

"Well…"

"Daisy, you're only torturing yourself," she griped, coming to stand beside me. "Everything will work out. You'll see."

"I'm sure it will." I paused and stared at the drawer, reciting the letter in my head again. "I just miss him."

She gave me a wry smile. "Absence and the heart, and all that. Right?"

I sighed. "Maybe."

"Get some sleep. You'll feel better. No dreams, right?"

I shook my head. "Just the one. I don't feel one coming tonight, though I can't always tell."

"Well, I'm here—no matter what."

I nodded, "I know. Thanks."

I did dream as soon as I fell asleep, but it wasn't like the ones I was used to. It was like watching a movie.

Kristoff walked into the room just as Lucas was finishing filing paperwork.

"Hey," he breathed, "still at it?"

Lucas nodded. "Yeah. Any word?"

Kristoff pursed his lips. "No, nothing yet."

Lucas sighed, getting to his feet and stretching the kinks out of his back. "Will you even be able to tell me when you *do* find something?"

He nodded. "I've been permitted to tell you most of it. It's Mother, Lucas. She's yours just as much as she's mine."

He nodded. "Good."

"What about you?"

He met his brother's eyes, and he had that accusatory look I had seen before. "What *about* me?"

"How are you, Lucas?"

"I'm—fine. Fine."

"Fine? You don't seem fine. You're—distracted."

He shook his head. "Don't do this, Kristoff. Please."

"Lucas, you need to talk to her."

"Not yet," he disagreed. "Not until I know it's safe."

"I talked to The Order. They don't know her memories have returned. They have no idea that everything is like it was before."

"Shouldn't they be aware of everything, Kris?"

He narrowed his eyes. "Don't go there, man."

"Kristoff, they didn't know about that man; the one who died. How did they *not* see that coming?"

"I don't know, Lucas. Why didn't *you*?"

"I…"

"A lot of what The Order knows comes from your dreams. Without them, much of it comes as a surprise."

"That's my point. They should know everything. You know, Kristoff. You *know* they aren't who they claim to be."

"And what do you suppose we do about that? Create more hysteria? Start a war? Throw all our secrets out to an unsuspecting world, threatening our very species? You tell me, Lucas."

He huffed. "So, we have to listen to them?"

"We have to stay out of their way," he said. "At least for now."

"For now?" he questioned. "What does that mean?"

"It's easy for me to gain inside knowledge and stay aware of their plans of action. If I suspect there is *any* way to stop them without endangering everyone else, I will let you know. Then, and only then, will we do…something."

He nodded. "Fine. Then just—keep me posted."
He nodded. "Of course. And Lucas?"
"Yeah?"
"Talk to Daisy," he said. "You'll be safe, I promise."

Chapter 4

I AWAKENED GROGGY. *The nurses had sedated me when I started screaming. I rubbed my eyes again, but something was still very wrong. I felt like I was trapped in an old black-and-white TV show. What was wrong with my eyes? I started panicking again but didn't want to be knocked out. I pressed the call button and I was already in tears when a nurse came in.*

"What do you need?" she asked. "Are you in pain?"

I shook my head and tried to reply but my voice was caught in my throat. I struggled for a few moments until finally I could say a couple words.

"My eyes..."

The nurse approached me and shined a flashlight into my eyes.

"Umm...I'm going to get the doctor," she stated.

"Wait," I called, "Please, tell me what's wrong."

"I have to get the doctor," she placed a caring hand on my arm, "I can't be sure."

"That's why I was screaming," I replied, "I can't see..."

She cut me off, turning to walk back to me. "You can't see?"

"*No...I mean...I can't see...color.*"

"*She frowned. "Okay, I need to get the doctor.*"

"*I didn't argue but I could tell it was something serious. When the doctor came in, he asked me a million questions that I didn't know how to answer. When he realized how frustrated I was, he took a deep breath and blew it out. "Let's start again. Explain what has you so upset.*"

"*Something is wrong." I rubbed my eyes for the umpteenth time. "I can't see color.*"

"*What colors can't you see? All color?*"

"*Yes. Everything is...gray.*"

"*Monochromacy," he murmured to the nurse.*"

"*Mono what?" I urged. "What is that? What's wrong?*"

"*Monochromacy," he repeated. "Try to stay calm, Daisy. With this kind of head injury, it's not uncommon for people to suffer vision impairment.*"

"*Vision impairment. Meaning what?*"

"*Okay, look, with the injury to your head, the cones in your eyes could have been damaged. In most cases, victims of similar injuries lose their sight entirely. If you can see at all, you're very fortunate. We'll run some tests, an MRI and a vision analysis. Monochromacy is a condition that occurs when there is damage to the retinal cones in the eye. It can occur after stroke, illness, or—like in your case—severe head trauma.*"

"*It can be fixed, right? You can fix it?*"

"*The doctor sighed. "Daisy, Monochromacy is almost always irreversible. I'm so sorry, but it can't be fixed. You're lucky you can see at all. Try to stay positive. I know it's hard...*"

"*You're supposed to be a doctor! You're supposed to help me, to make me better.*"

"*You're alive, Daisy, and you're not blind. I'm sorry, I am, but I'm going to call this one a win.*"

"*You have to do something.*"

"We'll run some tests. Let me just make sure I understand. Your vision is in gray scale, correct? Black and white."

I nodded.

"We'll figure it out. I just want to prepare you for the possibility that what you're experiencing is permanent."

I looked away. "Where's my mom?"

He smiled but it was forced. "She's right outside. Do you want to see her?"

"Please."

I barely recognized my mom when she entered the room. Her dark blue eyes, her most memorable feature, were muted and dull. I could tell she had been crying.

She rushed to my side. "You're awake. Are you in pain? Do you need anything?"

"I'm just a little sore," I tried to reassure her but I couldn't stop the tears from falling.

"Then why are you crying? Don't be scared. The doctor said you're going to be okay."

"It's not that."

"Then what? Talk to me, Dais."

"Something's—wrong. With me."

"No, baby. There's nothing wrong with you."

"No, Mom. You're not listening. There is something very wrong."

Her eyes became distant, but a look of concern crossed her face.

"My eyes…" I couldn't get the words out.

"You can see, can't you? You seem to be looking at me, can you…"

"I can see," I audibly swallowed, "but everything is…gray."

"Gray? What do you mean?"

"In gray, Mom. It's all in gray."

Chapter 5

"IT SEEMS PRETTY unlikely that anything has changed." Her eyes became suddenly distant.

"What?" I cooed. "What's that look for?"

She shook her head. "It's nothing," she sighed. "It's just…I hate seeing you like this. I hate that I'm your best friend and I can't do anything to help you."

I immediately mirrored the lost look on her face. "You help me by being here, Jess; by believing me."

"It's hard not to believe you. With how much I remember and everything that went along with it…"

"I know. Still."

She nodded. "Don't lose hope. Okay?"

"I won't. I—can't. It's still unlikely that we can be together. I mean—if The Order forbids it or even disapproves of it, it's too dangerous to even try."

She nodded. "But he loves you," she mused, "and everyone knows you love him. I know you think love isn't enough, but… maybe it is."

I sighed. "I want to believe in the whole 'love conquers all' thing but it's almost impossible after what we've been through."

She rolled her eyes. "Tell me about it."

I huffed out a breath. "At least the dreams have stopped for a while."

Jess nodded. "Yeah, that's good."

I could hear boredom creeping into her voice. We were both tired of talking about the same thing. Still, it was difficult to not steer the conversation back to our situation whenever we talked about anything.

"Can we try to *not* talk about it?" I asked. "I mean—let's go back to the café and talk about unimportant things."

She smiled. "I would love to, but I honestly don't think there's a way to avoid the topic. Until we get some answers, our minds won't let us."

I groaned. "Yeah, you're right."

Jess twisted her lips to one side. "Why don't you try talking to him?"

I tilted my head with a sigh. "You know I can't."

"I don't mean go to his house out in the open. Why can't you two talk? You know—like the way he talks to you."

"You mean in a dream?"

"Yeah. Have you two ever tried that before?"

I hesitated for a moment. "Well—no. He always comes to me in dreams. I don't know if I can do the same."

"I think you could," she said. "You obviously have a connection. If he can do it, maybe you can too."

I thought about it for a moment, almost afraid to accept the possibility. Getting my hopes up might leave me feeling defeated later. I knew I should tell her about the dream I had of Lucas and Kristoff, but I wasn't ready yet. I hadn't even decided what I thought it meant. I was sure it wasn't *just* a dream. I wasn't that lucky.

The night was warm and quiet. My mind was still and centered. I didn't feel that unsettling tug of an oncoming dream. I tried to breathe slowly and deeply as I fell asleep, reaching out to Lucas in my mind.

I slipped into a dream. It felt completely natural. Everything was in technicolor, so I knew I was asleep. I was at the park where I kissed Lucas the very first time. Sitting tentatively on the bench, I waited to see if he would find me. I pulled my sweater tighter across my chest. I wasn't startled when I felt a soft pressure on my shoulder because I knew he was there.

"Daisy?"

I turned around, meeting his beautiful, hazel eyes.

"How—did you do this?"

I shrugged. "I don't know. I just thought of you as I fell asleep."

He smiled. "Seems like it's easier for you than it is for me. You really are something else."

I smiled back. "We're connected."

He hung his head. "I'm sorry I haven't come to see you yet."

I blinked away tears. "Lucas, I miss you so much."

He sat beside me and wrapped me in a hug. "I'm sorry for the way things are right now. I'm trying to find a way to fix it."

I leaned back a little. "To find a way we can be together?"

He brushed his fingers through my hair. "Yes," he said. "I promised you I would find a way."

"There's only one way, isn't there? We can only be together if The Order can be disbanded once and for all."

He sighed. "It's beginning to look that way, yes."

"Lucas, it isn't possible. They're too powerful."

"No," he murmured, "they're not. They want us to believe they are but it's just not true. Kristoff is a member now and has gained a lot of influence and inside knowledge. If he can find a way, he promises he will take action."

I sighed. "*If.*"

"Really. We've been talking and he doesn't trust them either."

"Did you—give me a dream the other night by any chance?"

He narrowed his eyes. "What are you talking about?"

"I don't know," I mused, looking away. "I had a dream about you and Kristoff talking about The Order."

He raised his eyebrows. "Last night?"

I nodded.

"That—wasn't me. It must have been Kris. Damn, I should have known."

I tilted my head. "Known what?"

"Remember that gift I told you about? How Kris can give you ideas?"

"That was *him*?"

"It's part of what he can do. That encounter actually happened, but he allowed you to see it while you were asleep. You're more susceptible to his influence when you're sleeping. He wanted me to talk to you, but I was too scared."

"Well?"

"Well, what?"

"He promised it was safe, didn't he?"

He shook his head. "Yes, but I don't know I can trust it yet."

"You can trust *him,* can't you?"

He crossed one leg over the other. "Well yes, of course. I'm just…nervous."

"So am I, but I have to see you, Lucas. I'm going crazy."

He leaned forward and kissed me lightly on my forehead. "You're seeing me now."

I rolled my eyes. "It's not the same."

He was silent for a moment. "I know."

"Then just come to me. Please."

He sighed lightly. "Okay." He pulled away and looked into my eyes. His lips curled up into an almost smile.

"Okay what?"

"Okay, I'll come see you."

I smiled wide, feeling butterflies in the pit of my stomach. "Really?"

He nodded. "Really."

"Good."

"So, you're okay being together like this until then?"

I smiled. "Of course."

When I awoke, my excitement was too much to contain. I shook Jess awake. "What?" she groaned, opening her eyes halfway.

"He's coming to see me," I sang.

She murmured with a yawn. "Lucas?"

"Duh."

She rolled over and groused, "Good. Go wake *him* up."

I chuckled and went to get ready. I was sure he would find me—all I had to do was wait.

Chapter 6

"IT'S BEEN SIX MONTHS," *I said.*

Mom furrowed her brow. "Still no change?"

"You know what the doctor said, Mom. It's irreversible. I'm not going to get better."

When tears formed in her blue eyes, I soothed, "Mom, I'm okay. Really. It's been an adjustment, but I'm fine."

She smiled, but it didn't reach her eyes. "Are you?"

"Yes," I replied automatically, "I am. I'm alive. The doctor even said it's a miracle I'm not blind. Do you know how rare that is? We should be looking on the bright side." The words stung my mouth as they came out, but they had to be said.

Though I believed it, I wasn't exactly as okay with it as I pretended. I just couldn't let my mom lose it like that. I really was okay. I just wanted her to be okay too. Seeing me like this couldn't have been easy but I needed support, not sympathy.

"I don't want to make things harder for you, but I can't help but hope you'll get better. Is that okay? Can I hope?"

"It's counterproductive if it's false hope," I said.

"I want you to get better. I don't want to stop wanting that for you."

"I don't need to get better, Mom. I'm still me. I'm still Daisy."

She moved closer to me on the couch and pulled me close. "I know you are," she soothed, kissing the top of my head. "Just tell me again that you're okay."

"I'm great," I said.

"You are." She answered matter-of-factly.

I smiled at her usual loving words. She always made me feel like I was worth it. Even now that I was 'broken' she still loved me. Love was what I needed, but I did notice she looked at me differently now. There was sadness, sympathy, and guilt in her gaze—all the things I didn't need any more of. I couldn't hold it against her, but it hurt. It hurt me because now I wasn't the only one suffering.

Chapter 7

"CARE TO EXPLAIN how you did that?"

"Did what?" I asked, innocently, though I knew what he meant.

"When I come to you in a dream, it takes everything out of me. I'm exhausted afterwards. But you? It almost seemed natural."

I shrugged. "I don't know. I just…did it."

He pursed his lips. "That's helpful."

I smirked, nuzzling into his chest. "I've missed you."

He leaned against me, returning the affection. He moved away and looked into my eyes. "I have news."

"What kind of news?"

"Well, good news. For me, more like amazing."

I smiled. "Well, tell me before I die from the suspense."

"You know how Jess usually remembers me? Because of your connection?"

"Sure."

He shifted more towards me. "Well, it turns out it's more than that."

"What do you mean?"

His face lit up. "Truth is, I think people *can* remember me now; and I mean *everyone*."

I raised my eyebrows. "Seriously?"

"It seems that way. I talked to Moe and Kristoff. They claim they didn't know, but apparently, Mr. White put some sort of…curse on me. He didn't trust how rebellious I was. I guess he thought I wouldn't be a threat if I had no chance at a normal life, and then maybe I'd be willing to join The Order."

"So why has the curse broken?"

"I'm not sure, but it's probably because Mr. White is dead. We think my mother killed him. I guess when he died, the curse died with him."

I wrapped my arms around his shoulders. "That's so amazing, Lucas. I'm happy for you."

I felt his phone vibrate in his pocket. He sighed heavily, moving away from me. Unlocking his phone, obvious annoyance flickered in his eyes. "Hello?"

I couldn't hear who was on the other end, but Lucas immediately perked up.

"What? When?" He eyed me, grinning from ear to ear. "Yeah, of course. I'm on my way."

My heart sank when I realized he was leaving.

He ended the call and rose to his feet. "That was Kristoff," he said. "They found my mother."

I couldn't stop from smiling. I knew how much she meant to him.

"I'm sorry, Daisy—"

"It's okay," I interrupted. "Go."

He gave me a sorrowful look, then leaned down and kissed the top of my head. "I'll be back."

I nodded. "I know." I watched him walk towards the door, wishing I was going with him. "Lucas," I called.

He turned to glance at me. "No, Daisy. Stay here. I promise I'll be back."

I sighed and approached him. "Please? I can stay with Kristoff, can't I?"

He shook his head. "No, you can't, Daisy. Kristoff and I are in this together."

"I'm a part of this," I argued, "I deserve to be there. We're in this together too, Lucas. You and me. Always. Remember?"

He sighed and pulled me into a hug. "I just want you to be safe."

"I'll be fine," I mumbled into his chest, "but I refuse to stay here. I'm coming with you."

He pulled away and looked me hard in the eyes. "Fine, but if I tell you to stay put…"

"I won't move an inch. Promise."

He pursed his lips. "Come on," he sighed.

I smirked in triumph and followed him to the car.

"I don't like this," he said and then muttered to himself, "Kris is gonna kill me."

"Oh please, he knows how stubborn I can be."

Lucas chuckled halfheartedly.

I buckled up and glanced over at Lucas, who was staring at me. "What?"

He shook his head. "Nothing. I'm just amazed by you. Even when you're being impossible, at least you fight for what you want."

I smiled. "I guess I do."

"I'm only taking you with me because I feel I can protect you if I you're nearby. You haven't won."

I chuckled. "Uh huh."

"I'm serious."

"Do you—" I faltered. "Do you really think I won't be safe?"

"Kristoff says The Order is unaware that your memories came back and everything is like it was before, but I have no way of knowing that for sure." He continued more calmly, "No, I don't think they would come after you; but if I have to leave for any length of time, I need to know you're protected —at least for my own peace of mind, if nothing else."

I paused to take it all in. "Are you sure?"

"Does it matter?" he asked, amused. "You were dead set on coming with me, and now you care what I think?"

I shrugged.

"You're a pain in my ass."

I shrugged. "But you love me."

He shook his head. "Yeah, yeah. You're still a pain in my ass."

"Right back atcha, sweetheart," I teased.

He glanced at me with a grin, then focused on the road. I laughed at his inability to throw something witty back at me.

"Does this mean I won this one?"

He grunted. "Sure, Daisy. You won this one."

I smiled and nestled down in my seat.

We pulled up to the house and I immediately felt a pang of anxiety.

When I walked in, it almost felt like I'd entered a past-life. A dreamy sensation of déjà vu flooded over me as a collage of memories flashed through my mind. I pressed my fingers to my temples, to calm my brain.

"You okay?" Lucas asked.

"Yeah," I said, looking up at him. "Fine."

He squeezed my hand. "You sure?"

I nodded. "Yeah, I'm okay."

Kristoff stepped into the room dressed in the same dark blue suit he'd worn when we went before The Order to convince them to let me live. My heart literally ached, and I felt almost sick at the memory.

"Great," Kristoff spat. "She made you bring her, didn't she?"

"You know how she is," Lucas said. "She made a good point, Kris. I promised her I would keep her safe. This is how."

"This is different, Lucas. She is *our* mother. This has nothing to do with Daisy."

"Not true," I interrupted. When both men merely stared at me, astounded, I continued, "I mean yeah, she *is* your mother, but it doesn't have 'nothing to do with me. Don't forget for one minute that I'm a part of all of this. You can't keep me in the dark."

Kristoff ran his hands through his hair, frustrated. "Daisy, Lucas was too scared to even *see* you until today. And now you want to put yourself into the open like this?"

I looked him right in the eyes. "I am not afraid."

"You should be," he retorted, throwing his hands up. "Lucas, please. Back me up here."

"She's right, brother. I'm sorry. I don't like it either, but I don't feel right leaving her behind. I feel better knowing where she is 'cause she'd be in twice as much danger if I left her behind."

"See? I'm safer with you. If that's not a good enough reason, I don't know what is."

Kristoff huffed. "Fine, but I don't like it."

I nodded. "Noted."

Blowing out a breath and shaking his head, Kristoff murmured, "We don't have all the time in the world, so are you two ready?"

Lucas nodded. "Yeah. Where climbed?"

"According to Moe, she's In Portland?"

"Portland?" I echoed, surprised. "Like…as in Oregon?"

"Yes, Daisy," he mocked, "Portland 'like as in Oregon'."

"It's okay," Lucas whispered to me. "It's not that far."

"I need to text Jess."

"Right," Lucas murmured, "I forgot about that."

I grabbed my phone out of my bag to see she had already tried getting a hold of me. I had two missed calls and a text message.

(Jess) where'd you go? I came back downstairs, and you were both gone.

I decided I would just be honest.

(Me) Sorry, I'm with Lucas. I won't be home for a couple days, but don't worry."

She replied almost immediately.

(Jess) My mom isn't going to like that. You promise you're okay?

(Me) Yes, I'm safe.

(Jess) Okay. Keep in touch so I don't worry.

(Me) I will. I'll be back soon, I promise."

I closed my messages and shoved the phone into my back pocket. "Okay," I announced, "let's go."

Kristoff slung a duffle bag over his shoulder and walked past me toward the door. He shot me a glare, but I ignored him.

Lucas grasped my hand. "It's a long drive," he said.

"I'm aware, Lucas."

He shrugged. "Okay, then. Just remember, you wanted to come."

I narrowed my eyes but didn't say anything. He was going to love this. I climbed into the back seat, beginning to experience some minor anxiety. I didn't dare let Lucas see it. I couldn't risk him changing his mind and leaving me behind. I tried to regulate my breathing and sit still. He turned to glance at me. I faked a smile, which seemed good enough for him, and Kristoff started the car. He was still silent but the stiffness in his shoulders and death grip on the wheel spoke volumes. I hated him being mad at me.

"I'm sorry, Kristoff" I said. "I know you don't want me here, but please don't be mad at me."

"Daisy, I'm not mad at you."

"You are, I can tell."

He sighed. "I'm not. I'm just worried that you may—get in the way. I don't mean that like it sounds, but I can't worry about you and the job at the same time."

"I won't get in the way, I promise."

"That's not what I mean. It's nothing that you may or may not 'do.' It's just you being there. I can't have any distractions."

I tried to think of something to say.

He continued. "Just do as I ask and stay behind when I tell you to, okay?"

"Of course," I said. "I'll do whatever you say."

"Good."

The drive was brutal. Fifteen hours in the car. Even the short breaks for snacks weren't enough to keep the soreness and cramps in my legs at bay. It was almost midnight when we finally got to Portland. Lucas was asleep in the front seat, but unfortunately I hadn't been able to rest. Kristoff had turned off the music an hour ago and had not bothered to say one word. I was bored out of my mind and sighed in relief when we finally pulled up to a motel.

I leaned forward in my seat. "Are we staying here?"

"Just for a few hours," Kristoff replied. "We'll leave first thing in the morning."

He shook Lucas awake and he stumbled out of the car, stretched, and then walked to the motel office. Kristoff only got one room, so Lucas and I had to share a bed. Not that it was a problem, but I felt very awkward in a room with Lucas when Kristoff was just a few feet away from us.

It was either the exhaustion from being stuck in a car with no sleep or being wrapped in Lucas's arms, but for some reason I didn't dream.

Lucas shook me awake. "Come on, Daisy."

"It's still dark," I groaned, forcing myself to sit up.

"We have to go. She's waiting."

"Your mom?"

"Just get up, Love."

I obeyed and rushed through a quick morning routine, which Kristoff still seemed to think took too long.

He drummed his fingers on the night table. "Can we leave, already? We're going to be late."

"I'm ready," I sneered. "Relax."

He sighed, holding open the motel door. When we all piled back into the car, I felt the cramps almost immediately creeping into my legs again.

"It's not far," Lucas said, almost as if he had read my mind.

He was right. The drive only took about twenty minutes, and the sun was up by the time we pulled up to the house.

The house was small but lovely. It had a large redwood door and bay windows. Moss and vines covered the trees in the yard. I had never seen so much greenery. I hadn't noticed it at all during the drive.

Lucas rushed out of the car even before Kristoff, and I followed them up the driveway. Lucas halted a few feet from the door. Kristoff turned back to him.

"Lucas?" Kristoff said. "What's going on?"

I glanced at Lucas and his face was blank; unreadable. "Hey," I breathed. His eyes suddenly focused but he still looked lost, almost defeated.

"Are you okay?" I asked, trying to remain calm.

"Uh—yeah," he said, slightly shaking his head. "I'm just…tired."

I nodded, unable to hide the suspicion on my face.

"Promise," he said. "I'm fine."

I grabbed his hand and tugged him towards Kristoff, who was at the door. I kept my eyes on Lucas for a moment, but he seemed almost like himself again.

"Don't say a word," Kristoff ordered, eyeing me.

"Sure." I pretended to zip my lips and throw away the key.

He inhaled slowly and knocked on the door.

I waited, the tension emanating from Lucas was palpable. I tightened my grip on his hand, but he pulled it away. The door opened just a crack, and Lucas inhaled sharply.

"Kristoff?" The woman's voice wavered.

She opened the door farther, revealing her face. She was young, possibly in her thirties, with jet black hair and eyes that appeared to be hazel. She reminded me of Lucas.

"Aunt Kathrynne," Kristoff said, moving in for a hug.

Kathrynne slightly sobbed in his arms and moved to Lucas, pulling him into an even tighter embrace.

"Oh god, it's so good to see you. You're both so handsome."

I smiled, feeling very out of place. I realized it was wrong to intrude on their intimate family moments like this.

"And who is this?" She asked, moving away from Lucas and staring intensely into my eyes.

"Kathrynne, this is Daisy," Lucas said. "She's very important to me, so make her feel welcome."

"Well, aren't you pretty?" she said and gave me a gentle hug.

It threw me off guard but I returned it anyway, trying not to express how uncomfortable I was.

"Where is she?" Kristoff asked.

"For heaven's sake, boy, can't you come in for some tea first? I haven't seen you in years."

"I'm sorry," he said. "I am happy to see you, it's just…"

She smiled but it was obviously forced. "I know. I understand. Come in and we'll talk."

I followed them into the house. Across from the small, tiled entry was a decorated living room. There were flowers everywhere, some in vases and others in pots. Even the wallpaper and carpet had floral patterns, all in dark colors—possibly maroon and burgundy. It felt classy and sophisticated. Kathrynne sat on a floral couch and gestured for us to join her. There was a metal tea pot on a tray with beautiful ceramic cups. Were we in the 1950s? It all seemed a little strange, but then nothing about Lucas or his family was normal.

Kathrynne reached for the teapot and filled four cups. "It really is good to see you," she said. "I know you want to know about your mother."

Kristoff perked up. "Where is she?"

"She's here…" she said. "Well, not *here* here, but she'll be here."

Kristoff stiffened. "When?"

She glanced at her watch and shrugged. "An hour or so, I think."

"What do you mean?" Lucas demanded. "Where is she?"

"Would you relax?"

"Relax? I haven't seen my mother in god knows how long. How can we relax?"

"She'll be here," Kathrynne. said almost soothingly, "I promise. She wants to see you."

Kristoff answered, "Can't you tell us…?"

"No," she interrupted putting her hand up. "She asked me not to. She will explain everything to you herself."

The boys quieted down. I sipped my tea, only enough to be polite. I felt like I should say something but realized saying nothing would be more appropriate at a time like this.

"Why don't we talk until she gets here?" Kathrynne said.

"About what?" Kristoff asked.

"Like, how you are?"

He sighed but Lucas elbowed him lightly in the ribs. "We're—fine," he croaked and cleared his throat. "I just attended my banquet for joining The Order."

"Oh, is that so? I wish someone told me. I would have been there."

Lucas deadpanned. "Trust me, you didn't miss a thing."

"We know how you feel about The Order, Lucas, but it's important to your brother."

Kristoff laughed. "Actually, this time he's right. It was pretty dull."

She smiled. "Well…" she broke off averting her eyes. "I'm sorry about what happened to you, Lucas."

He looked into her eyes and cleared his throat. "Yes, well Mother took care of that."

Kathrynne blew out a sigh, "It doesn't make it okay."

"I know," he choked out. "I tried telling you before. They're evil."

She didn't reply but an annoyed look played across Kristoff's face. It was gone as soon as it appeared, making me wonder if I had imagined it.

Kathrynne avoided eye contact with me. She must have known who I was; that I was the reason Lucas had been tortured. I didn't blame her for not wanting anything to do with me. I had caused enough trouble already.

An awkward silence that filled the room, and the feeling that I should say something filled me but, for the life of me, I couldn't figure out what that might be. Lucas looked at me with an almost defeated expression. I reached for his hand but he pulled away. I tried asking him about his reaction with a confused look on my face, but he looked away. I wondered if maybe Kathrynne wasn't aware of who I was after all, and Lucas intended to keep it that way. I relaxed, trying to remember that Lucas loved me. He promised he would always love me. What was happening had nothing to do with us.

The next hour felt like days. There was hardly any conversation, save for one-line comments and even shorter responses. When there was a knock on door, both Kristoff and Lucas were on their feet, racing to answer it. I didn't get up for fear of intruding on their reunion. I peeked around the corner. Both the boys were in the arms of a woman I assumed was their mother. She had tears streaming down her pale face. Her dark lashes were wet, making them appear as though they sparkled. She opened her eyes and, even though everything was gray, I could tell they must have been a dark, cobalt blue. She caught sight of me and locked her gaze with mine before pulling out of their embrace.

"You must be Daisy," she said, taking a few steps toward me.

I tried to smile but wasn't sure if I did

"I'm so happy to meet you. I'm Margaret. You are very important to my son." Her voice was almost lyrical.

I tried picturing her as a bear, shredding Mr. White to ribbons. It was impossible. She was too beautiful. Her hair was dark like Kathrynne's, but I could see Lucas had her smile and nose. Kristoff definitely had her eyes, though. Before I could think of something to say, she was pulling me into a hug. I tentatively returned it, unaware of how I was supposed to feel.

She pulled away and Lucas came to stand beside me, his eyes moist with unshed tears. I followed them when they moved towards the living room.

They sat down on the couch, and Margaret grasped Lucas's hand. "Ah, my boys," she said, "I missed you so much."

"Where were you?" Kristoff asked, sounding almost angry. "Where have you been all these years? We thought you were dead."

She bowed her head. "I know," she solemnly replied, "I was trying to protect you."

"From what?"

"From everything," she snapped, and then took a deep breath and continued more calmly. "The Order for one. And your father and I weren't getting along, so I knew things would only get worse if I stayed,. I messed up. I know I did."

"But...Mr. White," Lucas said, "You killed Mr. White."

"Yes. I may have left, but I was always close by, keeping an eye on you. I knew what he did to you. Nobody hurts my baby and gets away with it."

I shuddered at her words, realizing she may just be as brutal and unforgiving as The Order. I still couldn't speak and felt like I should. I sighed, trying to calm my nerves. I could almost feel the emotions pouring off Kristoff and Lucas. They were angry at her for leaving—that was obvious and under-standable—but more than that, I could feel the love and the joy that was overflowing. It was actually comforting seeing them all together.

Kathrynne still wouldn't look at me, but Margaret smiled at me a few times, unafraid to make eye contact. I wondered if she knew I was to blame. She killed Mr. White, but would she kill me too if she knew it was all my fault? Before the thought was able to cause me any anxiety, she answered me, almost like she could read my mind.

"You know I don't blame you, Daisy. Right?"

I faked a smile. "Thank you."

"What The Order does is never any one person's fault. They do what they do, and we stay out of their way."

Her tone was tense, and both Kristoff and Lucas looked away for a moment. There were obviously more conflicting opinions about The Order than just between the boys.

She cleared her throat. "Anyway. I'm just glad to be back with my boys again."

Lucas forced a smile but Kristoff completely broke eye contact and looked away. I could tell he was angry. I hated when he was like that. It always made me uncomfortable for some reason.

I leaned over, whispering to Lucas. "Is he okay?"

He whispered back. "He'll be fine. He's just—hurt. We both are."

I nodded, falling back into the uncomfortable silence.

There wasn't much going on that I could engage in. I answered the questions Margaret asked about my life and listened to the stories she shared about the boys' childhoods. She really did love them. She even managed to make Kristoff laugh a few times, which was nice to hear. He had this sweet-sounding, contagious laughter that always made others smile. I wished I had known Lucas when he was younger. I smiled and laughed with the others as they reminisced. I took a liking to Margaret. She seemed real and genuine, like Lucas.

Chapter 8

IT WAS late by the time we made it back to the motel.

"So why couldn't we stay again?" I asked.

"I told you," Lucas said, "Kathrynne doesn't like company."

"Kathrynne doesn't like *me*."

He pursed his lips. "Don't take it personally. She has a hard time. She and my mother both know The Order is evil, and Kathrynne just hasn't been able to get over what happened to me."

I hung my head. "She blames me."

He nodded. "She needed to blame someone."

I sighed, unable to argue. "I'm sorry," I said.

He smiled. "Daisy, don't do that. You already know I don't blame you. It isn't your fault—in any way."

I nodded. "Sure."

"You *know* it isn't. Right?"

I didn't reply. It didn't matter what he said, I would always feel guilty about what happened. It was hard knowing he went through all of that for me. That made it my fault, at least in one way.

We curled up in bed together. I focused on feeling him close to me, knowing he loved me. Whatever else might happen, he would figure out how to keep us safe.

The next morning, we immediately returned to Kathrynne's. Lucas was unusually quiet and barely engaged in conversation.

"We need to get back home," Kristoff said to Margaret. "I have a meeting and Daisy needs to get back before Jess starts to worry."

She nodded. "You'll come see me again though, right? I'll be staying at a hotel in Cayucos after tonight."

"Of course," he said. "We'll come to see you soon."

Margaret smiled sadly. "Okay. Drive safe; I'll see you soon."

Lucas remained silent and barely returned his mother's embrace. Something was going on. I'd never seen him like that before.

The drive home was the same. Lucas seemed checked out, lost somewhere in his head.

I leaned forward and asked, "Are you okay?"

He looked over his shoulder, his eyes finally focused. "I'm fine. Why?"

"You seem, I don't know, out of it. Detached."

Lucas shrugged. "I'm just tired, and seeing my mother was a little strange."

"I can't believe she thinks she can act all nonchalant and tell childhood stories about us like nothing has changed," Kristoff said. "Like she didn't abandon us."

Lucas sighed. "I know. She's doing her best."

Kristoff snorted. "A little too late."

I didn't say anything as it was obviously a sore subject.

Kristoff dropped me at home around noon the next day. He smiled and gave me a mock salute, but Lucas didn't even look at me. I figured he was just dealing with personal stuff and would talk to me later when he was more himself. I wasn't going to demand his attention when he didn't want mine.

Jess immediately ran to the door when I walked in. "Hey, are you okay?"

"You worry too much," I nodded. "I'm fine."

"Good. My mom hates when you leave like that. I never have anything good to tell her."

I shrugged. "As long as she doesn't try to stop me, it's okay."

"She loves you, Daisy. She really does, and she would definitely have more rules if she could. She just doesn't feel right trying to tell you what to do since you're eighteen."

"And not her daughter."

Jess pursed her lips. "I was trying not to say that. You are her daughter in a way; just like you're my sister." She smiled.

I stuffed my hands in my pockets. "Well, either way, you know there are too many things she can't know about."

Jess nodded with a snort, "She'd send us both to the nut house."

I grunted. "And then some. What *did* you tell her?"

Jess cringed. "The truth."

My eyes widened. "Jess! Are you serious?"

"I'm sorry," she griped. "I couldn't think of a reasonable lie she would believe."

I groaned, turning away. "God. She knows I was on a trip with my boyfriend? She's totally gonna think we're doing it."

Jess looked at me surprised. "Aren't you?"

I turned back to Jess and she was smiling, suppressing

laughter. I smacked her arm. "No. Not with his brother only feet away from us."

"But…generally?"

I rolled my eyes. "That's not the point."

"You're eighteen, Daisy. She would probably suspect it anyway."

"Still not the point, Jess," I grumbled. "I don't want to be in her face about it."

She shrugged. "Then don't leave again."

I glared at her. "Whatever."

"Come on," she crooked a finger. "Upstairs. I want to show you something."

I followed her to our room.

"Close your eyes," she said.

"Really?" I chuckled.

"Yes. Come on. It's a surprise."

I shut my eyes and I heard her open the door. I took a step forward into the room and waited.

"Okay, open them."

I opened my eyes and gasped. The room was filled with easels, stacks of canvas and paint.

"Oh my god. Jess…" I gasped.

She clasped her hands together. "You like it?"

"It's amazing, but—"

"Don't tell me you can't paint," she protested. "I know you can!"

She sat on her bed.

"This—this is too much."

"Don't worry. It didn't cost that much." Jess looked unconcerned.

I slowly shook my head in wonder. "Your dad is going to kill you."

She waved me off. "He won't care. It's for you. He'll only be mad if he thinks it's for me." She chuckled.

I took it all in and bounced on my toes. "Well, you did say you were thinking about art. I can give you some lessons. I mean, the color might be off but I can try. He doesn't have to know."

She smiled. "That would be great."

I hugged her and stepped back. "Thanks Jess. I mean, for the supplies but mostly for believing in me. I'm still not sure I can do this, but your support helps a lot."

She was still smiling when she replied. "What are you waiting for? Get started."

"Now?"

She raised an arm, palm up. "Why not? You got somewhere to be?"

I sighed. "I don't know…"

"Come on," she said, "I'll help you."

I thought a moment and nodded to myself. "Fine."

I grabbed one of the smaller canvases and attached it to the easel. Then I picked a paint pot but was unsure which color it was. I knew it was best to start with a landscape. Those were always easier, not as many straight lines or exact details like portraits. I picked up a brush and dipped it into the paint. I started feeling anxious and unsure, but it felt completely natural as soon as the brush touched the canvas. The movements started coming back to me. Each stroke took me back to before the accident, when painting was my passion. To before, when I lost all hope of being an artist. I smiled and continued with the base of a tree trunk. When I finished the tree and moved to the top to paint the sky with different shades of blue, Jess stopped me.

"Wait," she said, "Daisy, that's green."

I looked at the paint in my hand. "Is it?"

Jess nodded. "Dark green."

I sighed. "I thought it was dark blue." I looked closer at the bottle and, sure enough, it was labeled 'forest green.'

"Well, that's okay. Besides, the tree looks amazing."

"Does it?"

She nodded. "Yeah, you used different shades of brown and green and added shading. It looks great."

I sighed again. "This is impossible."

"It's okay," she said, "here." She handed me a different color. "Dark blue."

I looked at her for a moment. Her eyes held that familiar sparkle and she was smiling like she usually was.

"Okay," I murmured.

I continued with the shades of blue, glancing at Jess every few minutes to make sure I was using the right colors. When I was finished, I could tell it looked all right.

"Well?"

Jess had a huge grin on her face. "Wow."

"Really?" I was worried she was just being nice.

"I'm serious Dais, It's beautiful. I wish…" she broke off.

"What?" I asked.

"Nothing." Her voice was dull.

I understood, though. "You wish I could see it?"

"No," she said. "You *can* see it, you painted it."

I shot her a look.

"Okay, I *was* going to say that, but I didn't mean it."

I sighed dropping the brush. "It's okay."

"It really is great."

I tried to smile. "Thanks."

The next day, I looked at the painting again and wished I really *could* see it in color the way Jess could. I picked up the bottle of black paint and used a tray to mix it with various amounts of white. Painting in shades of gray was the only thing that made sense. At least it would prevent me from painting the sky green. I stroked the brush across the canvas, loving the feel of it. It had been so long since I had felt my passion for art. I began to see the details and the soul of what I was painting. It wasn't a lake and shrubbery. Well, it *was* those things, but it was so much more. It was like a warm Sunday afternoon or a cool dip in the lake under the summer sun. It was the feeling of the week's stress slip away. It was the love of the earth and a passion for simply being. I was painting life as it was now, and I lost myself in it as I always had.

When I glanced at the clock, I realized I had been at it for over an hour. Jess walked in and instantly raved, "Daisy that's…" she broke off, taking a step toward the easel. "Wow. I have no words."

"You have to say that," I said, smiling.

"No," she said, glancing at me and then back again at the painting. "I don't *have* to say anything. This is truly incredible. All in black and white."

"It's called monochrome."

Her eyes brightened. "I really don't know what to say."

"So, it's not dull?"

"Dull?" She shrieked. "Not even close. It's so beautiful. I wish I was there. Is that a real place?"

I shook my head. "Only in my head. I've always liked the lake."

She smiled. "You create worlds when you paint."

I mirrored her smile. "I guess that's why I love it so much. It can be whatever I want it to be."

Chapter 9

IT WAS late in the morning when I awoke after a surprisingly peaceful sleep to a knock at the front door. I perked up and pulled my hair back before rushing downstairs to answer it.

"Daisy," the way he said my name was almost frantic.

I stepped outside with him. "Kristoff? What are you doing here?"

"Something's wrong," he hesitated and then rushed, "with Lucas."

My throat tightened and my stomach dropped. "What do you mean wrong? Is he okay?"

He shook his head. "I don't know. He won't talk to me."

I narrowed my eyes briefly. "What do you want *me* to do?"

"I don't know.…try talking to him."

"If he won't talk to you, what makes you think he'll talk to me?"

He shrugged. "I don't know but I'm out of ideas. I know him, and something just isn't right."

I remembered his odd reaction after seeing his mom the day Kristoff dropped me off. I knew he was right.

"I noticed," I said, "I thought it was about your mom."

He shook his head. "It's more than that. I can tell."

I nodded. "Okay," I said with a sigh. "I'll try."

"Thanks, Daisy."

"But…if he won't talk to me, what else can we do?"

"Do you have a reason to think he wouldn't?"

I shrugged. "He's been really distant lately. I just assumed it was about your mom. Her coming back and everything has been really stressful—for both of you."

He dropped his head for a moment. "Yeah, it has. But I think there's more to it than that. If he won't talk to you, then I'll really be worried."

I nodded. "Okay. I'll see what I can do."

"I don't see what he's making such a big deal of," Lucas said.

"He's just concerned," I answered. "We both are. You've been a little distant lately."

"Daisy, it's been a rough week for me. For Kristoff, too. I'm fine, okay?"

"You sure?"

He nodded. "I've been a little tired lately and a little checked out, I admit, but it's nothing I can't handle. I'm sorry if you've felt neglected."

I scoffed. "I'm no schoolgirl demanding you spend every waking moment with me. I'm just worried about you."

"I know," he tucked my head under his chin, "but you don't need to be. I'm here and I'm fine."

I didn't know what to say. I still felt like there was something he wasn't telling me. He put his arm around me, and I leaned into him, sighing.

"Stop worrying, Dais."

I tried to trust him again but, no matter the situation, worrying was something I always had a tendency to do. I closed my eyes, focusing on the fact that we were together. I reminded myself how much that meant to me, remembering how hard it was to be away from him.

Lucas stiffened suddenly, and he didn't feel so warm anymore. I looked up into his eyes and he had that faraway look again.

"Lucas?"

He didn't answer, just stared off into space.

I shook him a little. "Lucas?"

He blinked his eyes rapidly and looked at me. "I already told you I'm fine," he muttered. "Let's go upstairs."

I was taken aback for a moment. "Okay, but why do you want to go upstairs?"

"It's more private."

He pulled me toward the stairs. "Jess is home," I said.

He stopped short. "Then her parents' room."

I shook my head. "I don't feel comfortable with that."

His eyes narrowed, and I saw a flicker of irritation. "What's your problem?"

"What do you mean?"

"Why are you trying to avoid me?"

"Lucas, I'm not avoiding you, I'm right here. Something is going on with you. Please just talk to me."

"I'm fine," he insisted. "I want make love to you, and you're pushing me away."

I put a hand on his chest. "It's not like that. I just want to respect Jess's parents. They took me in when I had nowhere else to go."

He looked away. "Well—they wouldn't know."

"*I* would know."

"Fine." He yanked away angrily. "Then I guess I'll leave."

I grabbed his arm. "Wait, you don't have to go."

He scoffed, "Why would I stay?"

I felt my stomach drop. "You only came over to…"

"Obviously," he spat and headed for the door.

Tears welled in my eyes. I didn't even try to stop him. I ran up to my room and threw myself onto the bed. Jess was in the armchair reading and immediately rushed to my side.

"Daisy, what happened?"

I couldn't speak so I just shook my head.

"Did you guys just break up?"

I shook my head again. "No," I choked, sitting up, "but it seems we might. I have no idea what's wrong with him."

I told her what happened, and she didn't interrupt. Making sure I was finished, she waited a moment before replying, "Well, that's…sleazy."

I nodded. "Right? But he was never like that before."

"You're right," she agreed. "That's weird."

"Exactly."

"So just to be clear, he came over here to…do it?"

I sighed. "Yeah."

She continued, "And got mad when you didn't want to?"

I nodded again. "Yeah."

"Okay, then. That's not like him at all. I'll give him a good kick in the nads if you want."

I shook my head. "No thanks. Contain your bitchy side for once."

She frowned. "Fine. What are you gonna do?"

I sat up. "I think I need to talk to Kristoff."

She nodded. "Okay. Good luck."

"I should probably wait until tomorrow, though, until I calm down. I really don't want to start crying in front of Kristoff."

"Are you sure I can't kick him? Just this once?"

I shot her a look.

"Fine," she threw up her hands. "Let's hang out until tomorrow. Get your mind off of it." She batted her eyes. "I got snacks."

I smiled. "Sounds good."

I just stared, waiting for Kristoff to answer.

"Are you sure you didn't misunderstand?"

I frowned. "What could I have misunderstood, Kristoff? I repeated our conversation verbatim."

He sighed. "It's just—not like him."

I raised my eyebrows. "Exactly."

He ran his hands through his hair. "I don't even know where he is right now."

"What do you mean? He never came home?"

"No, he came home," he answered. "He was—quiet. He left a while later, claiming he needed some air. I don't know where he went."

I nodded. "I do." I slung my bag over my shoulder and headed down the street.

I didn't reach the park until my feet began to ache. I saw him sitting on the bench, staring into space. "Lucas?"

He turned to look at me and a smile spread across his face

and he finally looked present. "You found me."

I smiled, sitting down beside him. "Of course, I did. Are you okay?"

He furrowed his brow. "What do you mean?"

"Lucas, you've been acting so…strange—"

"Daisy…" he interrupted.

"No," I retorted. "Don't 'Daisy' me, and no more lame excuses. What is going on with you? The truth!"

He sighed and dropped his head. "I—I don't know. Something doesn't feel right."

"What do you mean?"

"I don't know," he spat, frustrated. "I just—I'm confused, and there are chunks of time…missing. Like yesterday. I didn't even remember how I acted until this morning. Daisy, I'm so sorry. The way I treated you was inexcusable. You know it's never been about—*that.*"

I leaned against him. "I know. What got into you?"

"I really don't know what's wrong with me. I thought it was the stress with my mom and The Order and everything, but it's getting worse."

My stomach sank. If he didn't know what was wrong, I feared we may never discover how to fix it. I wasn't ready to lose him.

"Whatever it is, we'll figure it out," I said. "Why don't you head home? It's getting cold."

His grin was more of a grimace. "Sure," he nodded, "I'm just not looking forward to facing Kristoff."

"He's worried about you, Lucas."

"Yeah, but you know how he is. He's so—pushy. A little boorish at times, too."

I stifled a laugh. "I know," I replied, "but you can't avoid him forever."

"Says who?"

I chuckled. "Come on," I said. "Home."

Chapter 10

I WOKE *late in the morning and when I opened my eyes, I instinctively rubbed them. I grumbled and closed them again, deciding I didn't want to be awake yet. I didn't want to deal with this yet. A knock on my door clearly indicated I had no choice.*

"Daisy?"

I pulled the covers over my head. "Hmm?"

"It's almost noon."

I didn't answer.

"Don't you remember? You wanted to come with me today."

I pulled the blanket down. "With you where?"

She smiled. "July's wedding. Remember? You were persistent about coming shopping with me for the accessories."

I sighed. "Right."

"It's okay, Daisy. You can stay home."

"No," I answered, sitting up. "I want to go." This was my chance to prove to my mom that everything was fine.

I got up and rushed to get ready, trying my best not to focus too hard on anything. Especially my favorite dark blue sweater that didn't look blue anymore.

I met my mom downstairs, keys already in her hand. "Ready?"

I nodded.

We drove to the bridal shop. The puffy white dresses in the window were comforting. They were always white.

"The bridesmaids are wearing a powder blue," my mom mentioned. "I'm looking for ribbons to make sashes with. Something simple."

"Okay."

We went opposite directions through the store. I read every single tag carefully to make sure I was picking up the right colors. I met my mom back at the front of the store.

"I can't decide between a few," she said. "What did you find?"

I handed her the ribbons I picked up, different shades of blue.

"Hmmm."

"What's wrong?"

"Nothing. It's just—well, this one," she held one up, "Is too close to the actual color of the dress. The others are more—purple."

"The tags say blue."

"Yes but—they're more of a violet-blue."

I sighed.

"No, it's okay. We'll keep looking."

I already felt the sting in my eyes, and I turned away so she wouldn't see. I headed back to the ribbon section and picked out a few more.

My mom didn't say anything when I handed them to her. She glanced at me with a forced smirk.

"Also wrong?"

"No," she replied. "Of course not."

"Then…"

She shrugged. "Well, they're just not exactly the right shade—but they're close."

"What about this one?" I pointed to one on the rack.

"Purple? With powder blue?"

"It's purple?"

She nodded.

I was so frustrated, and angry, that the tears I'd been fighting spilled over.

"It's okay, Daisy. Look, I think I found something. Everything is fine."

Like ribbons were actually the problem. Everything is fine? I looked back to her and the expression of pity on her face made me feel almost sick. I rushed out of the store, ignoring her calls for me to come back. I just couldn't be there. I couldn't pretend anymore. I faced the brick wall of the building and sobbed like a child.

Chapter 11

WE WALKED IN BUT, just as expected, Kristoff stomped toward the door. "Lucas, what the hell?"

"Don't," he sighed, "I'm not in the mood."

"Not in the mood?" He echoed, tension rising in his voice. "I was worried sick."

Lucas thrust a hand through his hair. "I'm not a child, Kris. I can take care of myself."

Kristoff scoffed, "Oh yeah, I can see that."

"Just stop. I'm fine, okay? I'm just tired."

Kristoff glanced at me and raised his eyebrows, waiting for me to step in. I shrugged my shoulders, not knowing what to say.

"Has he at least talked to you?" he finally asked out loud.

I nodded. "We talked," I replied, "He's okay. I think he just needs some time to himself." The lie came out forced, and I was sure Kristoff noticed but he let it go.

"Fine," he said, "I'll leave you alone for now, but you are going to have to talk to me eventually."

Lucas waved him off, heading toward his room.

"I'm worried, Jess. Something is very wrong."

"What do you think it is?"

I shrugged. "I'm not sure, but it obviously has something to do with The Order."

"Doesn't it always." It wasn't a question.

I sighed. "Until they're ended, there's not much we can do. Kristoff is working on something. Hopefully, with Mr. White gone, he can gain enough credibility to at least change things. Maybe turn The Order more into what they claim to be."

Jess crossed her arms. "As long as they aren't hurting people, Daisy."

I shrugged. "There's nothing I can do about it, regardless. If they are keeping the balance, it can't be *that* bad."

"Keeping the balance means ending lives, doesn't it?"

"It can," I said, "but not always. They often save people."

She pursed her lips. "What they claim to be still hurts people."

"But if it's what's natural—"

"It's not," she interrupted, "Remember? For whatever reason, it's what they are *choosing* to do."

I sighed. "You're right," I agreed. "I hope whatever Kristoff has planned can stop the killing."

"And if it can't?"

"Then he'll figure out a way to make it stop. I don't know, Jess. It's not really my area of expertise."

She sighed. "I hate knowing what's going on and not being able to do anything about it."

I shook my head. "You and me both."

"So, what *are* you going to do?"

I shrugged. "I called Lucas. He said something about wanting me to know some things. I'm not sure what that's all about."

Jess exhaled loudly. "Fill me in later?"

I nodded, "Of course."

It took about twenty minutes for Lucas to get to my house. When he walked in, he looked disheveled and distressed.

"What's going on?" I asked.

He glanced at me, then looked away and went to sit on the couch. I followed. "Do you remember what I said about Kris wanting to change The Order into what they used to be?" He asked, his voice tight with worry.

I nodded.

"Well, I think I should explain something about The Order. Their agenda hasn't always been about keeping the balance."

I my stomach clenched nervously. "What are you talking about?"

"You were right, Daisy. The Order is not a group of all-knowing gods who maintain nature's balance."

I blew out the breath I'd been holding. "So, they are making these decisions themselves?"

He bowed his head. "Yes."

"How long have you known this?" The words came out harsher than I intended.

"I've suspected it all along," he said, defensively, "but I didn't know for sure. Not until Kristoff told me."

"Told you what exactly?"

He sighed before answering. "Back before my time, even before Moe's time, some humans were aware of us."

"Of what you were?"

Lucas nodded. "That's where werewolf and shapeshifter lore comes from. Unfortunately, not all the humans were as… understanding. Many of them feared us. Many of them killed us."

My eyes widened. "Oh my god."

"The Order was established as a way to protect ourselves. It was an alliance of shifters who were willing to fight for our right to live."

"So how did they become—this?"

"I'm getting to it." He grumbled. "Lots of fights and secret wars occurred between the humans and my kind. Unfortunately, humans can't fight lions and tigers—at least not without guns, which very few had back then. It turns out that those who knew about us were mostly killed and the others took the knowledge to their graves, leaving nothing more than 'fictional' stories behind."

"So how did The Order become what it is today?"

"When the younger members of The Order rose to leadership status, they fostered their hatred for humans as well as a desire for power. They used lies and scare tactics to convince us that theirs was the only way to keep the balance of nature and began killing humans they thought might suspect us. When I was born and my gift became apparent, they started using it to decide whether I was to save certain people or not."

"But why?"

He shrugged and began pacing. "Power, Daisy. They've been using me to prove they have the power to grant life or condemn beings to death. If all beings are afraid, then no one will question them. They *hate* humans—partly because of the ones that hunted us centuries ago, and partly because they view humans as weak and flawed. Inferior." He stopped short. "There is one more thing."

"What's that?"

"The Order is a large network. You know how I file for Moe, right?"

I nodded.

"Well, The Order pays its members, too. That's how Kristoff has managed to keep his house, even after Moe stopped paying for it. The problem with disbanding The Order is that we would all have to live among humans. Get jobs."

I wrinkled my brows. "What's wrong with that?"

"It risks our exposure," he growled, "and may very well mean creating another 'Order' to protect us from humans who would want us dead because we're 'different' or considered dangerous—which, let's be brutally honest, we sometimes are."

"How did they become so wealthy?" I asked.

He sighed. "I don't know, and I'm not sure we want to. Most likely insurance fraud, theft, or money laundering of some kind."

"Nice." My murmur was heavy with sarcasm

"I just thought you needed to understand some things. You're just discovering what I am. Everything Kristoff is permitted to tell you, at least. Some things, he's not."

"And what about you?" I asked.

"Me?"

"Yeah, how are you feeling?"

"Not sure," he said. "Better, I think. I haven't had any chunks of time missing recently."

"That's good. Let me know if you find anything out. Keep me in the loop, okay?"

"Promise." He said, smiling thinly.

Chapter 12

IT WAS EARLY when my cell rang, waking me from a particularly restful sleep. No dreams and no nightmares. I glanced at my phone. 6 a.m. I would have thought about ignoring the call, but it was Kristoff. He wouldn't be calling me if it wasn't important. "Hello?"

"Daisy?"

"Yeah. What is it?" I groaned.

"Sorry to wake you, but something happened."

I could hear the urgency in his voice and knew something was wrong. "Is Lucas okay?"

He hesitated and cleared his throat. "That sort of depends."

I instantly shot up. "On what?"

"On what you classify as okay."

"Is he hurt?" I demanded

"He's alive. Listen, we shouldn't talk about this over the phone. Can I come over?"

I looked at Jess who was still sound asleep. "Umm—sure.

Give me a few minutes though."

"Sure," he agreed. "See you soon."

I jumped out of bed and rushed through a shower. I didn't even bother to dry my hair, letting it soak the back of my shirt. Lucas was in trouble so there was no way I could relax until I knew he was safe and sound.

I waited on the stairs, staring out the window. I couldn't stop anxiously biting my nails and tapping my feet. When I saw Kristoff's silver car in the driveway, I rushed to open the door. "What happened?" I demanded, as he stepped inside.

"Daisy, breathe," he said.

He followed me to the couch and sat beside me. "We both know Lucas has been acting...strangely lately," he started.

I snorted. "Try nuts."

He nodded and shrugged. "That's appropriate, especially after his last little escapade."

"No..." I paused, taking a deep breath and trying to not lose it. "What did he do now?"

Kristoff cursed, surprising me, and then he complained through gritted teeth, "He not only acted like a child, he risked our exposure. You're not going to believe this but—Lucas was in a bar fight."

I was stunned. "What? A bar fight, like a drunken brawl?

He nodded. "He put the guy in the hospital."

I threw my hands up, exasperated. "Oh my god. Why the hell would he do something like that? I mean...the guy had to have threatened him, right? Lucas would never do that unless he had a good reason."

Kristoff shook his head. "From what I heard it was practically over nothing. I guess Lucas wanted the guy's chair and things escalated."

I rubbed the back of my neck. "That doesn't sound like him at all."

He threw his hands up. "Exactly. What the hell is wrong with him?"

I shook my head. "I have no idea. Have you talked to him?" I asked. "Has he explained why? I mean, he *had* to have a reason."

He rubbed his eyes, tiredly. "Daisy, if that were the case, I wouldn't be here."

I sighed heavily, turning away from him. "We have to ask him about it. For all we know, it's a huge misunderstanding."

"Some misunderstanding," he peeved, "he almost killed the guy."

I grabbed my purse. "I'll talk to him."

He cocked a brow. "Good luck finding him."

I looked back at him. "What do you mean?"

"I haven't seen him since last night." Kristoff shrugged. "I tried calling him and even tried looking for him. He doesn't want to be found."

I nodded. "I think I know where he is. I'll find him."

Kristoff exhaled audibly. "Okay," he finally said, but he still looked unsure.

"Whatever is going on, we'll figure it out. We always do."

I found Lucas at the park again, sitting on the bench and staring into space. He didn't acknowledge me when I approached him. "Lucas?" When I got no response, I clapped my hands in front of his face and yelled his name. Nothing. I sat beside him, put my hand on his shoulder, and shook him.

Startled, he practically jumped out of his skin. "It's okay," I said. "Just me."

He stared at me, confused. "Daisy?"

I raised my eyebrows, "In the flesh."

He rubbed the back of this neck. "I don't…how…"

I took his hand in mine. "Take your time."

He looked around. "How did I get here?"

"You don't remember?"

He shook his head. "How long have you been here?"

"I just got here, but you didn't hear me when I tried talking to you."

He took a deep breath and blew it out. "Just now?"

I nodded and he shook his head, averting his gaze to the ground. "I don't understand."

"Kristoff called me and then came to the house. He explained what happened, sort of."

Lucas was surprised. "My brother called you?"

I nodded. "He was just hoping you would talk to me. Tell me what happened."

He looked confused. "What do you mean?"

I rolled my eyes. "C'mon, Lucas, you know what I mean." When he shook his head, I prodded, "Last night. At the bar?"

His face pinched in confusion. "What?"

I put a hand on his shoulder. "Lucas, I'm not mad. Tell me what happened."

He slowly shook his head. "Daisy, I honestly don't know what you're talking about."

My blood ran cold. "You don't remember being at the bar?"

His voice raised. "What bar? What the hell are you talking about?"

"Apparently, you were at a bar last night and got into an —altercation."

"What altercation? With who?"

I shrugged. "I don't know, but Kristoff said it was bad. Lucas…"

"No," he murmured. "No…I couldn't have—"

Sensing his panic, I interrupted. "No, he's alive and stable, but he's hurt. He'll be in the hospital for a while."

Lucas's eyes burned with fear. "Daisy—I don't remember anything."

I inhaled to calm my nerves. "What do you mean?" I was afraid of the answer but had to know. "What *do* you remember?"

He shrugged.

"Lucas…"

He shook his head again, looking away. "I feel like I have been asleep for weeks and woke up here."

"That's all?"

"That's everything. That's all I remember."

"What do you think we should do, Lucas? This is not normal."

"I know." His voice was soft and far away but I could still hear fear behind his words. "I think I should talk to Moe. He might know something."

I nodded and stood to my feet. "Let's go, then."

"Now?"

I offered him my hand. "So you want to just wait for it to happen again?"

He huffed but took my hand and stood up. "Fine."

"I'll drive," I said.

We headed to my car, and Lucas seemed a million miles away before I even started the engine. He stared out the window, emotionless, as if he couldn't see what he was looking at.

I had a feeling he'd get worse if I pushed him, so I drove silently to Moe's.

After I put the car in park and grabbed my purse, Lucas sat still as a statue and continued staring out the window.

"Lucas?

When he didn't respond, I gently gripped his shoulder and he jolted like he'd been electrocuted.

"It's okay," I soothed. "It's okay. We're here."

He furrowed his brow, gazing around, confused.

"Moe's," I said.

"Oh…" he pressed his fingers to his temples. "Right. Sorry I…"

"It's okay. You don't have to explain anything. We'll figure it out."

Chapter 13

FOR A MOMENT HE JUST STARED, like he hadn't heard a word we said. "How long?" He finally asked.

Lucas and I exchanged a look. "A couple months," I said.

Lucas glanced at me again before speaking. "It started with just forgetting things but it's getting worse. Moe, I—I hurt someone."

Moe's eyebrows shot up. "You *hurt* someone?"

He nodded. "He's alive but it was bad. Serious."

Moe exhaled audibly and sat back against the couch.

"What?" Lucas asked.

Moe rose to his feet. Lucas followed him so I followed suit. Stopping at the hall closet, he pulled out a step ladder climbed up to rungs to reach the top shelf and then handed Lucas a hat box.

"What is this?" Lucas asked.

"Hold on," he put the ladder back and grabbed the box from Lucas. "I don't know if it's still in here."

We followed Moe back to the couch and he fumbled through the box.

"Ah," he breathed, pulling out an old leatherbound book. "Here it is."

"What is it?"

"Remember The Order always asking its members to keep a journal?"

Lucas nodded. "I did for a while."

"Well," he paused, handing the book to Lucas, "that isn't a new thing. Members have been keeping journals since the very beginning of The Order. This belonged to one."

Lucas opened the journal and I scooted closer to see. The first page had a name.

Property of Rebekah Black

I tried to speak but nothing came out. I didn't know what to say.

"Rebekah was your grandmother, Lucas…" Moe said. "Your great-grandmother, to be more precise."

Lucas's eyes grew wide, and he looked at me as if trying to read my mind. I shook my head, still at a loss.

"I read it years ago," Moe started. His voice was soft and far away. "I—I never realized it could be…"

"Could be what?" Lucas peeved.

"I don't know—genetic?"

I immediately felt anxiety crushing my chest. "Genetic?"

"What, Moe? What could be genetic?"

Moe shook his head and shrugged. "That's the thing. I don't know. In this journal, Rebekah mentions experiences of lost time and doing things she doesn't recall. Often times, very out of character behavior."

I nodded. "Exactly like Lucas."

"I really haven't been myself."

"What happened to Rebekah?" I asked.

"I don't know all the details but I do know she…died—before her time, as I understood."

Lucas tried not to react but I heard him gasp.

"I don't know what could be happening," Moe continued. "I know you won't like it but there is one thing I can try."

Lucas threw his arms wide. "At this point, lay it on me."

"I need to talk to The Order."

Lucas stiffened, "You're right, I don't like that idea at all."

"Yeah, but they might know something."

"But if they don't, and you tell them, they will definitely get involved. That's the last thing I want."

Moe nodded. "All right. Let me do some digging and see what I can find.. I can't make any promises, but I'll let you know and we can discuss how to approach The Order if I strike out."

Lucas fell back onto the couch. "Okay. I really don't want them involved. I don't trust them."

"I know," Moe agreed. "After what happened to you, Lucas, neither do I."

I grasped Lucas's hand and he turned to me. He forced a flaccid smile but it didn't last.

"It's going to be okay," I said.

He nodded. "Yeah."

"Really. We'll figure it out. We always do."

"I'll let you know if I find anything out," Moe said.

Lucas nodded. "Thanks, Moe."

"Should we read it?" I asked.

He turned to me. "I don't know."

"It might help."

"Probably not. Moe said they never figured it out. He said Rebekah…"

"I know," I interrupted, "but there still might be some clues he missed."

He nodded. "I guess we can try it."

I inhaled slowly and opened the book, terrified of what I may find.

November 12, 1903

I'm losing time. I cannot remember what happened last night. I must have wandered into a barn late in the night. The horses woke me at dawn.

I feel lost. Confused. As if I had been possessed and had no control over my own body. My brain is foggy, and I am frightened. If they find out what is happening to me, I could be in danger.

There are red smears on my dress. I fear it is blood yet I do not seem to be injured. Did I hurt someone? I cannot know. Perhaps I am going mad. Perhaps they will have no choice but to reprimand me, even if I do not recall what I have done.

We were silent for a moment, just staring at the page.

"They?" I mused.

"The Order," Lucas retorted. "I am sure of it."

"Would they really banish her?"

He shook his head. "It'd be worse than that. Think about it, Daisy. If she hurt or killed someone—anyone—an investigation could've risked exposure. The Order would not, *could not*, stand for that."

"So, they…"

"Yes," he interrupted. "I can't know for sure, but it seems more than likely The Order had her…taken care of."

"They killed her."

He nodded. "They had no choice." He turned to the next entry.

November 14, 1903

It has happened again, only this time I seem to remember more than before. I remember stalking a young woman. I followed her from the tavern. I'm unsure why I was drawn to her or why I felt such a sense of rage toward her.

I had a knife hidden in the belt of my dress. I do not know where I got the blade or why I had it, but I do know I planned to use it. I planned to kill her.

Something stopped me—I don't know what. I still only know minis-cule pieces of what happens during my blackouts or why.

I awoke at home this time, which is more reassuring. The blade is clean, and I do not appear to have blood on my clothes. I do not remember coming home, but I do not think I hurt that girl. I pray I am right about that.

"That's even more strange," I said. "She remembers things but didn't before."

"That happened to me too, remember? I have no memory of the bar fight, but I remember being a total jackass to you. It took a while, but it came back to me."

I nodded. "This is so strange."

The next entry was a little more jumbled.

November 16, 1903

I lost time again. All of yesterday this time. Every moment since the time I awoke in the morning until I awoke today. I am covered in dirt and my hands are sore. I do not know what happened or what I did. I am confused. I want to tell Errol, but I am frightened of what he may do. He called to me so I believe he cares for me, but will it be enough?

"Errol," Lucas mused.

"Do you know the name?"

"My grandfather."

"Your grandfather?"

He nodded. "It's a family name. What if Rebekah wasn't my relative? What if Errol was?"

"Moe said *she* was, right?"

He nodded. "He could have been wrong."

"It wasn't an uncommon name back then, was it?"

He shrugged. "Maybe not. I'm not sure."

"I think we should talk to Kristoff."

Lucas's face pinched in annoyance. "Why?" His voice swelled with sarcasm.

"Well, he's in The Order. You said yourself, sometimes he knows things you don't."

He sighed. "Maybe."

"Can you be any less enthusiastic?" I wasn't joking but a chuckle escaped anyway.

"It's not funny," he peeved.

"I know. I'm sorry. You're attitude toward your brother is amusing sometimes. Just talk to him, please."

"I might not need to. I need to talk to Moe first and find out what he knows before bringing Kristoff into this."

"Into what?" we heard from the doorway.

I looked up to see Kristoff marching toward us. "Into. *What?*"

"Nothing," I blurted. "Really. It's not what it sounds like. We're just talking about…"

"About how I'm feeling," Lucas interjected. "I know it

concerns you, so I just thought we didn't need you to hear about it."

"Uh huh," Kristoff mused skeptically. "Whatever. I'm going to bed."

I glanced at Lucas and we both stifled laughter.

Chapter 14

THEY MADE *me stay overnight in the hospital but I only had strings of nightmares. None of them made sense, but they left me feeling even more tired when I woke up.*

Once they knew I was out of the woods, they let me go home. I just stared out the window at all the familiar streets and houses that now looked completely alien. Tears rolled down my cheeks, but mom didn't say anything.

I didn't want to talk or eat. To avoid anything my mom would likely ask me about, I hurried up to my room as soon as we stepped inside. Alone in my room, I hid my face in the pillows, trying to not look at my now ruined surroundings. I sobbed hysterically before falling asleep.

I knew I must have been dreaming when I opened my eyes because I did not recognize the area and it was all in color. It looked like an old, rundown apartment complex. The structure was covered in dirt and graffiti, and many of the windows were broken out and covered with tarps. I figured it had to have been condemned and had no idea why I would be here, even in a dream. I squeezed my eyes shut and opened them again to try and wake myself up. It didn't work. I shook my head. Nothing worked. I didn't want to be here. I shouldn't be here. I couldn't decide why I felt so scared and unsure. I just knew, I needed to get out of there somehow.

I turned away, walking another direction. I jumped almost a foot in the air when a thunderous popping sound reverberated through the complex, the windows rattled in their frames. I heard the sound again, loud enough now to hurt my ears. **Gunshots.**

My blood turned to ice in my veins, and I began to panic. I sprinted from the area as fast as my legs would carry me, my breathing labored and my heart pounding in my ears. I screamed, finally waking into the dull confines of my room. Drenched in sweat, my heart was still pounding. I sighed and rolled over. That was weird.

I stumbled into my bathroom to splash water on my face, hoping it would help ease the anxiety left over from the dream. It didn't. I hurried through my morning routine and headed downstairs

"Good morning," my mom said like she did every morning. It definitely didn't feel like any other day. "You okay?"

I met her eyes, and she stared at me, concern etched on her face. "Yeah," I said quickly. "Just had a weird dream."

"I know things are going to be different, but it'll end up okay."

"I'm just tired."

"Are you sure that's all? You seem—scared."

"It was kind of a scary dream but I'm fine. I promise."

She nodded, looking unconvinced. "Okay. Well, I'm heading out. I'll be back around seven."

I forced a smile. "Have a good day."

She left through the back door, and I headed toward the refrigerator absentmindedly. I pulled out a bottle of orange juice and clicked on the TV.

I froze, dropping the unopened orange juice on the floor and falling onto the couch behind me. I stared at the words "Breaking News" across the bottom of the screen. I felt like I had been transported into an alternate dimension. There on the screen was the apartment complex I had seen in my dream. It was exactly the same, from the broken-out windows to the graffiti sprayed across the walls. The only thing different was that I wasn't seeing it in color. I reached for the remote and turned up the volume.

"It is unclear at this time whether or not this was a murder or a drug deal gone awry. We are not ruling out gang activity but cannot confirm anything until a full investigation takes place."

I still felt like I couldn't breathe, and my heart pounded in my ears so loud I could no longer hear the TV. I raced back up to my room and fell onto my bed and pressed my face into a pillow. What was happening to me? Why was I seeing things from my dreams? It seemed taking the color from my life wasn't enough of a punishment. Whatever I did to deserve this, I don't know. I could just hope it was a onetime thing.

Chapter 15

"LET'S see if we can find out more from the journal," I said.

Lucas nodded and turned to the next page. "Whoa!"

"What is it?" I asked, leaning over to look at the page. "What the…?"

The page was covered in letters but not words. Not words that could be read anyway. They were scattered in circular patterns and spirals.

"Okay, that's weird," I said.

Lucas flipped through the book, finding much of the same insane word-filled swirls and whorls with letters so tiny it was impossible to read.

"That doesn't make sense," he said soberly. "Rebekah was losing time, but this?"

I could hear the fear in his voice. "Lucas, that doesn't mean the same thing will happen to you."

"Yes, Daisy, I think it does."

I grasped his hand and he sighed deeply. "We definitely need to talk to Moe."

I nodded, wanting to comfort him but unsure how when I had the same anxieties.

Lucas stood, and I could almost see him shaking. I followed, not saying a word. We got in the car and drove back to Moe's.

As soon as Lucas's father opened the door, he knew something was wrong.

"Moe, have you ever read this all the way through?" Lucas asked, handing over the journal.

Moe pursed his lips.

"You knew," Lucas spat.

"I was hoping maybe you could figure out what it was about." Moe rubbed the back of his neck.

"What *what* was about? This?" He turned to one of the crazy pages. "Why? Because I'm crazy too?"

Moe shook his head. "Of course not. That's not what I meant."

"Why would you think I could decipher…*this*?"

Moe turned away. "I don't know. I was just hoping maybe there was some pattern I just couldn't see myself."

Lucas raised his eyebrows. "I don't think so. It all seems completely random."

Moe ran his fingers through his hair. "I stared at it for hours. That's the same conclusion I came to."

"Moe…who is Errol?"

He stared at Lucas for a moment.

"You said Rebekah was our relative. Grandfather's name was Errol, wasn't it?"

"Well yes. But Lucas, it was 1903. It wasn't an uncommon name."

"No?"

He shook his head. "What are you trying to ask me?"

"If maybe you could be wrong. If maybe the Errol mentioned in the journal could, in fact, be my grandfather."

Moe's face fell. "I never considered it…"

"Where did the journal come from?"

"My mother, your grandmother gave it to me. She said it belonged to a Rebekah and she was a family member. She wasn't exactly clear about how she got it, and I was too young to realize I should have asked. Actually, I had forgotten all about it until a few months ago when I reorganized the closet. I found it in an old box. Strange how that happens."

"So that's it? There's nothing else? No other journals? Letters?"

Moe shook his head. "As far as I know, that's all that survived."

Lucas sighed, "Great. So, we have no idea what's happening to me?"

Chapter 16

ANOTHER DREAM HAD *me up a little earlier than normal and on my way to wherever my feet decided to take me. I pulled on my blue cardigan and sneakers and headed down the streets. It was cool, Autumn on the way.*

I knew I was meant to be at the lake but wasn't sure where it was. My body's autopilot took me where I needed to be. I approached the banks and scanned the water. Nothing yet. I waited, knowing I had to be ready. When I heard the cries, I sprang into action. I followed the sounds of splashing on the other side of the lake, but it was silent when I got there. I peered down and saw her. A little girl, quickly sinking, hands reaching for the surface.

I dove in, grasping her around the waist. She was almost weightless in the water, but I had a hard time getting both of us to the surface. I pulled with all my strength until I broke through the surface of the water. I held the girl's head up as I dragged us to the bank. I heaved her up out of the water. She was conscious. Thank god.

Water spewed from her mouth and she rolled over, coughing. I knelt by her side. She looked at me wide-eyed.

"Are you okay?"

She nodded. "I can't swim," she said.

"You need to stay away from the water," I urged. "Where do you live?"

She pointed behind her to the left. I looked through the trees and saw a house. It was close.

"You should go home," I said.

She nodded. "My mom will be mad."

"Your mom will be happy you're okay. Now, go."

She nodded and got to her feet. She wobbled for a moment and I placed my hands on her waist to stabilize her. I watched until she reached the house. Once she was inside, I turned back toward home.

My phone buzzed in my pocket. I checked the screen.

(Jess) Hey! Coffee?

(Me) You're an addict.

(Jess) Is that a yes?

(Me) Fine. Order me a mocha, I'll be there in 20.

(Jess) You got it.

I backtracked home and changed out of my wet clothes, towel dried my hair as best I could and headed to the café. I had no idea how I was going to explain this one to Jess, but she needed to know. More importantly, I needed to tell someone.

Chapter 17

I SAT ON MY BED, waiting for her to say something. She glanced up at me but was still silent.

"Please say something," I said.

"I'm still processing. I don't really know what to say."

I sighed. "I know. It's crazy."

"You'll figure it out."

I scoffed. "This isn't failing a math quiz, Jess. This is…"

"Huge," she interrupted. "I know."

"I'm scared."

She moved from the chair to sit beside me. She opened her mouth to speak, but a knock on the bedroom door stopped her.

"Your mom?" I mouthed silently.

She shrugged and got up to open the door. "Mom? What are you doing home?"

I leaned forward trying to listen.

"I'm taking some vacation time. Can I…?"

"Oh, yeah," Jess nodded, "come in. What's going on?"

"I actually wanted to talk to Daisy," she said, meeting my eyes.

"Oh, okay. I can wait downstairs," Jess answered.

"No, no, it's not like that," she said. "You can stay. It concerns you, too."

I furrowed my brow. "What does?"

"It's up to you how much you want to share but you and Jess have always been so close…I think you may need a friend. I have something I was asked to give to you some day in the event of…of your mom…"

"Dying?" I stated.

She nodded. "I waited a while, thinking you needed some time to heal."

She had a wooden box in her hands with a small, silver lock. I inhaled, trying to think of what to say. "Did my mom give this to you?"

She nodded. "A long time ago. I've never looked at it. I promised I wouldn't. I don't know what you'll find. If you don't want to see it, I understand."

"No," I retorted, reaching for it. "I need to, even if it's something I won't like."

She handed me the lockbox. "Okay. I'm going to be downstairs if you need anything." Her eyes bore into mine for a moment before leaving the room.

I stared at the box in my hands, my senses heightened. I could feel the coolness of the wood and the weight, but I didn't move.

"Dais?" Jess sang. "You okay?"

Her voice snapped me back to reality. "Yeah, just…I don't know what to think…"

She nodded. "I get it. Do you want me to leave?"

I shook my head. "No. I definitely don't want to do this alone."

I heard her inhale at the same time I did. I flipped the little silver lock, the quiet tick boomed like thunder in my ears. I envisioned the kinds of terrible things might be hidden inside: vials of blood, death threats from a masked villain, fossilized bones. I shook my head, trying to dispel the images from my clearly, overactive imagination.

I lifted the lid and was met with a thick stack of what looked like paper. I furrowed my brow and glanced at Jess. She shrugged. I picked up the paper on top and turned it over. It appeared to be a legal document of some kind from the county clerk's office, but I couldn't understand what was written. I handed it to Jess.

"It looks like a marriage license," she said.

"That would make sense."

"It says Donna and David Carmichael."

She handed it back to me and I saw the names. "Right."

"What else is there?"

I picked up the next paper I realized it was actually an envelope. I turned it over and my heart plunged into my stomach. Heat rushed to my cheeks.

"Dais?"

I glanced at Jess with tears filling my eyes.

"Diasy, breathe. What is it?"

"It's—" I swallowed. "It's...her handwriting."

"Your mom?"

I nodded, staring at my name written on the envelope. I never realized how well I recognized my mom's handwriting. Not until the very moment I saw it again. I pulled up the tab, careful not to tear the envelope. I feared I could be ripping to shreds, the last part of my mother I had left.

"It's a letter," Jess whispered.

I read it out loud. "Dearest Daisy. If you're reading this, it means I am gone. I hope you are all grown up now with a home and a family of your own. If you're not, I want you to know you will be okay. You are strong, and you will make it. My leaving this life was meant to be, and it's okay.

I know you have questions, and you will find them in the box this letter was in. I love you, Daisy, more than you will ever know. Your father loved you, too. You were our whole world. Nothing will ever change that! No matter what.

Your loving mom,

Donna."

"No matter what?" I mused, the tears now streaming down my cheeks.

Jess shrugged. "Moms say things like that all the time."

I shook my head. "I don't know. I'm scared to know what she was s hiding from me. Maybe I don't want to know."

"Well…we don't have to…"

"No," I exclaimed, then took a breath and continued more calmly. "No, we definitely do."

I ruffled through the papers and found something even more confusing. My hands shook as I read out loud, *"Certificate of Live Birth September 23rd, Baby girl Knox and Baby boy Knox, Born to Mary Knox.*

"What?" Jess asked

I handed her the paper.

"Oh my…" her words were breathy and wobbled. "Daisy, do you think…could you…"

"Have a brother?" I choked. "I think so."

"This is crazy."

"Jess…there's no father listed and…Mary was not my mother."

"Maybe it's a mistake. It could even belong to someone else."

I shook my head. "Why else would it be here? The letter said I would find answers. I never questioned who my mother was—until now."

She shrugged. "Just saying."

I shuffled through the rest of the papers. "These are all old school records. Report cards and a few research assignments. I can't believe my mom saved these."

"Wait," Jess cooed, "What's that?" She pointed to a stray paper.

I grabbed it. "It looks like a…death certificate for…"

"David Carmichael."

"My dad," I whispered.

"What does it say?"

"That he died of a heart attack when he was twenty-six."

"Is that right?"

I shrugged. "It's what my mom told me so, I'm assuming so."

"Are you okay?"

I shook my head. "I don't know. First, I find out my mom might not be my mom, no idea who my dad is… or was, and now I could have a brother too? *Should* I be okay?"

She sighed. "I'm sorry."

"No, I'm sorry. I didn't mean to snap. I just… I don't how I'm supposed to feel right now."

She swung her arm around me. "You don't need to figure that out right now either."

"Thanks."

"Hey, I got you a present." I could hear the forced cheer in her voice. She slid off the bed.

"A present?"

"Well…it was for both of us, but I think you need it more than me right now."

She reached under the bed and pulled out a bottle of red wine.

"Jess!"

She laughed. "Relax, my mom probably won't come back up here for the rest of the day. She knows you need to process all of this your own way."

I nodded. "What the hell, right? My world is falling apart, I might as well be drunk."

"That's the spirit," Jess laughed.

She actually had a corkscrew this time, so it was easier to open.

"Hmm," she hummed.

"What?"

"I don't know. I kind of miss finding creative ways to open a bottle of booze."

I laughed, finding myself agreeing.

"Do you want to talk about it?" Jess asked. Her voice was soft, as if she was afraid to ask.

I shook my head. "I don't know. I don't really know what to say. I'm still reeling."

"I know," she sighed. "Look…your parents…they *were* your parents, Daisy in every way that matters."

"I know that, I do. But it's not that simple. I mean, my mom named me after her favorite flower. So, whoever Mary was might have named me something completely different. It's an identity thing. I've always been Daisy Mae. What else did she lie to me about?"

"I'm sure she was just trying to protect you."

I nodded. "I get that, but it wasn't her decision to make. I had a right to know."

"Daisy, I think she planned on telling you when you were older. She just never got the chance."

"I don't want to be mad at her."

"Don't feel guilty for feeling the way you feel."

"Thanks, but I can't help it."

"Well, I know this sounds crazy so I'll shut up if you tell me to, but your mother—I mean, this Mary person... Do you think you might want to talk to her?"

I gasped. "Oh I...didn't even think about that."

"Bad idea?"

"No, it's not that. I just didn't even consider it with all the other crap going on in my head."

She nodded. "So?"

I ran through all the thoughts in my head, trying to detangle everything and decide how I felt.

"I think, yes. Eventually."

"Yes, you'd want to meet her?"

"Yes, but don't hold me to it. I'm still not sure how I feel."

"Got it. I'll be here for you. The whole way.

"Thanks, Jess."

Chapter 18

IT WAS A HOT, *summer day and the sun was a bright, orange ball in the sky. I didn't even care that it hurt my eyes to stare into it. The colors were too beautiful. I walked along the sidewalk, savoring the warmth. The flowers in the gardens I passed were vibrant and crisp.*

I jumped, turning around rapidly as a screeching howl thundered through the air. A truck careened down the road, completely out of control. That was when I saw the man. He was young, probably mid-twenties, headphones on, not paying a bit of attention to the road behind him. I didn't even have a moment to think, I reacted, reaching the street and screaming, "Hey! Get out of the street!"

He couldn't hear me but I kept shouting, running toward him as the truck drew closer. I felt its rumbling through the soles of my feet, but the stranger in the road remained oblivious. I approached him as the truck came dangerously closer. I tried picking up my pace but was already moving as fast as I could. My lungs burned but I didn't stop.

"Move!" I shouted. "Hey! Get out of the road!"

He still didn't turn around and I knew it was over. A flash of color filled my vision and the vehicle collided into me. My body burned and ached as its weight crashed into me. I felt as if I had been broken into pieces. Every cell stung. It didn't last long before I became completely numb.

Before everything went dark, a familiar face appeared, one I remembered from the day I wrecked my car. It was him. *The one who saved me. I tried to reach for him, tried to ask him who he was. How could he be here? WHY would he be here? No matter how many times I tried to ask, I could not speak. He was real—he had to be. I didn't care what the cops said. He was here in front of me, more real than my memory of him. His light hazel eyes and shaggy chestnut hair. He was real.*

I shot up in bed, practically screaming and drenched in perspiration. Another nightmare. But it couldn't be like the last one, right? I mean, that was just some crazy coincidence. It couldn't be more than that. I just needed to calm down and forget about it.

Going out seemed like a good way to clear my head but I couldn't stop thinking about the dream. I walked down the sidewalk, staring at the flowers and wishing them to change.

A screeching wail stopped me cold in my tracks.

No way. It can't be.

There was the truck. THE truck. And the man? I knew it was him, even without his bright red headphones. This couldn't be happening again. It just couldn't. But the truck was moving, and I didn't have time to debate. I sprang into action, terrified of what might happen to me. I was petrified at the thought of being crushed alive, but I was even more afraid of what would happen if I did nothing. So I ran, shouting and screaming at him like I did in my dream, only this time he turned around. His eyes grew as wide as saucers when he saw the truck barreling right for him.

I picked up my pace, running as fast as my legs could carry me until my muscles burned. The truck roared past me, the wind it displaced blew my hair into my eyes. Unable to see, I crashed into the man in the road, knocking him back onto the sidewalk.

My heart pounded in my ears. My body quaked with fear and adren-

aline. The man I just saved said nothing at first. He just stared, wide-eyed, practically in tears.

He stammered a few words. "How…? You saved…"

How could I possibly explain to him how I knew he would be here? He would think I was crazy. Hell, I thought I was crazy.

"Thank you," he whispered.

I nodded, still trying to catch my breath. I turned to leave.

"Wait," he called.

I turned around and his hand reached out to me. I couldn't explain myself because I didn't know how to process my feelings. "You're welcome," I murmured, turning away again.

He begged for me to wait but I ignored him. I had to figure out what was happening to me before I could try to explain it to anyone else. I knew there was only one way that could be. I had to find him. It was the only option I had.

Chapter 19

I HAD SO much to process with the new information, I almost forgot everything going on with Lucas. I had no idea how to navigate all of this. With or without Jess's support, it was just… too much.

A walk around the block was the best way to clear my head but it didn't seem to help. I stepped into the kitchen to see Jess's mom doing dishes at the sink. She turned toward me. "Hey."

I smiled but didn't know what to say.

"I don't want to pry but are you okay after what you found?"

I furrowed my brow. "Did you know what was in the box?"

"Absolutely not." she replied. "I promised your mom I wouldn't look. I just knew it was something important. We don't have to talk about it if you don't want to. Just know, if you need an adult, I'm here for you. It's my honor to take care of you like your mom wanted."

"Thanks. I'm okay but I do have one question."

"What's that?"

"Do you know why my mom named me Daisy?"

Carol smiled; her eyes sparkled. "Donna always wanted a Daisy. Since high school."

"Really?"

"Didn't she tell you?"

"She told me they were her favorite flowers."

Carol nodded. "Yeah, they were. She always said if she ever had a daughter, she would name her Daisy. I'm not sure where she got your middle name from though."

I nodded. "Thank you for telling me that."

"Are you sure you're okay?"

I smiled. "I'm fine, thank you."

I briefly considered mentioning the possible adoption but wasn't comfortable answering the plethora of questions she would ask.

I rushed upstairs before she had time to say more. Jess was sitting in the armchair with a glass of wine. She reached toward the other side of the chair and handed me the other glass. "You okay?"

"I'm still fine," I said. "I need to talk to Lucas but I'm having a hard time wanting to talk to anyone about this. I'm sick of talking about it."

"Maybe just take a day. We'll hang out here and talk about other things."

"With wine."

She lifted her glass. "Obviously with wine."

I laughed. "Sounds like a plan."

The next morning, I awoke with a throbbing headache. I groaned.

"Me too," I heard Jess say.

I rolled over. "How much did we drink?"

She reached toward the floor without shifting her weight. "Whole bottle."

"Figures." I sat up and a wave of nausea sent me sprinting to the bathroom.

I heard Jess giggle from the other room, but she wasn't far behind.

"Karma," I moaned as she lifted her head from the sink.

"Bite me."

We washed up and spent the rest of the day lounging in our room. Jess barely moved from the armchair, and I was still lying in bed until noon.

"You feel like coffee?" Jess asked, breaking the silence.

I groaned. "Kind of, but I'm not going anywhere today."

She scoffed. "Me neither. No farther than downstairs, anyway, I'll bring you some."

I smiled. "Thanks."

She headed toward the door a little slower than usual and being alone forced all the thoughts I'd been ignoring flooding back to me. I reached for my phone on the nightstand. I saw Lucas had tried calling me and had texts from his brother.

(Kristoff) Daisy, something is going on with Lucas again. Call me.

(Kristoff) Where are you? I have my lunatic brother on lockdown here.

Jess walked into the room. "I put hot cocoa mix in it," she mused.

I sprang from the bed, forgetting about the previous lethargy. My adrenaline was on overdrive. "No time," I said.

"What?"

I handed her my phone,

"Oh…got it. Go. Call me if you need me."

"Thanks." I grabbed my sweatshirt and raced out the door. I texted Kristoff on my way.

(Me) Hey, sorry, I didn't hear my phone. I'm on my way.

(Kristoff) It's okay, just hurry.

I practically ran down the road, completely ignoring the cold and the descending fog. I got to the driveway and Kristoff raced outside to meet me before I even got to the door.

"He's gone," he said, frantically.

"What?"

"I went back into his room, and he wasn't there."

I sighed. "How could he have gotten out? You said you had him on lockdown."

"I didn't mean I had him handcuffed to the bedframe or something, Daisy. Though at this point…"

"No, it's okay. I know where he is. I'll find him."

"He's not himself right now. I can't even get him to visit with our mom."

"Does she know?"

He shook his head. "I want to tell her, but Lucas begged me not to. Moe doesn't want her to know, either. We may have no choice at some point because she might know something that could help him."

I nodded. "Let me talk to him and see what I can do to convince him."

"He's not thinking straight."

"I know. It's okay."

He inhaled then nodded. "Keep me updated?"

I placed a reassuring hand on his arm. "Of course."

I turned and headed the opposite direction toward the

park. By then, the fog had lowered, obstructing the road in front of me. It swirled and danced almost menacingly as I trudged forward.

I knew he was there, even though he was shrouded by the mist. I slogged through the grass, feeling the bottom of my pants getting soaked.

I sat on the bench beside Lucas without saying a word.

"I don't know how I got here, Daisy," he whispered.

I looked at him, but he had his head down, staring at his folded hands.

"I know."

Finally, he looked up. "What's happening to me?"

"That I don't know, but we'll figure it out."

He pulled me into an unexpected tight hug.

"I promise," I whispered.

"I love you," he murmured. "It's the only thing getting me through."

I leaned away so I could look him in the eye. "I'm not going anywhere, Lucas. Ever."

His hand cupped my face, and then he sighed and stood. "We should get back. Kris is probably having a meltdown."

I tried to stifle the chuckle that slipped.

He pursed his lips. "Great. That's why you're here, isn't it?"

I shrugged. "He means well."

"Yeah, I know. I'm not mad. I just—I don't like putting him through this either."

I nodded. "Whatever is happening is not your fault."

He didn't reply. He grasped my hand, and we headed back toward his house. The mist was thick and unnerving, but I always felt safer with Lucas beside me.

Chapter 20

I AWOKE *that morning with the realization I hadn't dreamed. I was grateful for that, but it didn't help me figure anything out. I had to talk to someone about this. I knew I couldn't tell my mom. She would have me committed.*

I reached for my phone on the nightstand and called Jess.

"Daisy?"

"Yeah, I'm sorry. Were you sleeping?"

"It's 6 a.m."

"It is?"

I moved my phone from my ear to check the time on the screen. "Crap. I'm sorry. It didn't even register…"

"It's fine. Are you okay?"

"Is it that obvious I'm not?"

"Daisy…you're up at six o'clock in the morning. That's even more unusual than me being up this early."

I sighed. "Okay. I need to talk. It's important."

"Okay."

"I mean in person. This is…"

"Huge?"

"Yeah. Pretty much."

"Meet me at the café?"

"Sure."

I got ready as fast as I could and slipped out the door, hoping my mom wouldn't notice. I saw the driveway was empty, meaning she had already left for work.

I walked quickly, rehearsing in my head what I wanted to tell Jess. No matter how many versions I went through, they all sounded crazy. "She's going to think I've lost it," I whispered to myself. I sighed and picked up my pace. "I have. I've lost it."

The café was empty when I walked in except for Jess. I had forgotten how early it was.

"Hey," I said, sitting across from her.

"Hey. I got you a mocha."

"Oh, thanks."

"Don't mention it."

The awkward silence that followed only made my anxiety worse, but I didn't know how to begin.

"Daisy, are we going to talk about coffee? Maybe you can start with why you woke me up at the asscrack of dawn."

I smirked. "I'm sorry about that. I don't know what's happening to me."

Her eyes grew wide. "Happening?"

I nodded.

"Like…currently?"

I nodded again.

"Daisy—talk to me. Tell me exactly what's going on."

I looked away. "You're going to think I'm nuts."

"That's okay. I already think you're nuts."

She was smiling but irritation rocked through me.

"I'm sorry. Bad joke. Bad friend."

That time, I smiled. "Honestly, I probably am *nuts."*

"You're not crazy, Dais."

"That almost makes me feel worse."

"How so?"

"I've been having these—dreams."

"Like nightmares?"

"Worse."

"Like what?"

I sighed. "You won't believe me."

"Daisy, you called me to talk to me about it, didn't you?"

She was right, but I found myself instantly regretting calling her. Jess was all I had. If she thought I had a screw loose, I had no one.

I sighed. "It's not even the dreams that are the problem."

"Then what is?"

I paused, searching for the right words but couldn't figure out how to begin.

"Daisy? What is *the problem?"*

"The fact that they're…coming true."

The shock on her face was evident. "Come again?"

"See? I told you it was crazy."

"It doesn't mean YOU are."

"So…you believe me?"

She was silent for a moment. "I do, but…"

"But what?"

"I need a little more to go on, Daisy. Tell me everything."

"How many times has this happened?"

"The dreams?"

"I mean how many times have they come true? Could it be a fluke?"

"A fluke?"

"Like a onetime freak occurrence."

"No, I know what a fluke is. It can't be. It's happened twice now."

"Oh."

"Any ideas?"

"I'm sorry, Daisy. I've got nothing."

"There is one more thing."

She raised her eyebrows.

"Remember the guy I told you about, the one who pulled me from my car?"

"Yeah, I thought you said he wasn't real."

"No, the cops said he wasn't real. Doctors, too. I know he was."

"What about him?"

"Well…he's in my dreams, but it's weird. He's not really a part of them. He's just there in the background like he's watching it unfold."

"That's…creepy."

"To say the least."

"So, you think he has something to do with it?"

"Or he knows something."

She nodded. "We need to figure out why this is happening. This is all new, right?"

"Everything was normal before the accident."

"Normal is relative."

"Well, I wasn't questioning my sanity then."

"Point taken. I'll hit the books and let you know if I find anything."

Chapter 21

THE TENSION back at Lucas's was practically tangible. I wanted to tell him about what was going on with my family and about my possible brother, but I couldn't lay that on him now. Not with what was going on with *him*. At least not until things calmed down a bit. He usually knew when something was up, but he seemed too disoriented to pick up on it in his current state.

"I hate what I'm doing to you, Daisy," he murmured.

"I already told you; this isn't your fault, and I don't blame you for anything that's happened. This is being done *to* you."

"I know."

"There is something I wanted to ask you."

He looked at me with an accusatory expression.

"Don't panic, I just thought maybe you could ask your mom."

"My mom? About what's happening to me? Daisy, she'll flip out."

"Maybe not," I answered. "She's one of you. She might know something."

"I don't know."

"Try?"

"Daisy, after what I'm putting my brother *and* my father through—what I'm putting *you* through—you think I should lay this on my mother, too?"

"Well…yeah. We're your family, Lucas. Your struggles are our struggles. That's how it works. Let us be here for you. Let us help."

He nodded. "I'll think about it."

I blew out a relieved breath. "That's all I ask."

"If she can help, maybe it's worth a shot. But is it worth the risk of her being—terrified?"

"I think your mom is stronger than you give her credit for. She can take care of herself."

He raised his eyebrows. "Well, you're right about that."

"So?"

He sighed. "Okay…I'll do it."

"You'll talk to her?"

"I will. But I should get some sleep first. I don't want to go over there looking so exhausted."

"I understand." I pulled him into a hug. "Call me tomorrow."

"I will."

He kissed me briefly and headed to his room. I felt a sense of hope I hadn't felt before. I had a good feeling about telling his mother. I knew something was going to come from it and just hoped it was something good. I wasn't sure I could handle anything more that wasn't. We all needed a win.

The morning came full of stress, anxiety and uncertainty. Nothing was clear anymore. At least there were no dreams or premonitions looming. At least not yet.

"Everything okay?" Jess asked as I sat up.

I scoffed.

"Sorry. I just mean…"

"No, I know. Everything *is* a mess, but no dreams."

She nodded. "I'll go get us some coffee." She kicked off the covers and headed downstairs.

I lay back down, trying to decide what to deal with first. My phone buzzed, making the decision for me. Lucas. I pulled if off the charger.

"Hello?"

"Hey, it's me. I was wondering if you'd come with me today."

"Come with you where?"

"Umm…to see my mother. Remember?"

"Oh…right. Are you sure you want me there?"

"I'm not even sure I want to go at all. It's too hard to do this on my own and I can't put it on Kris."

I nodded though he couldn't see. "Sure. What time?"

"Give me a couple of hours to gather myself and I'll pick you up."

"Sounds good."

"Thanks, Daisy/"

"Of course."

Jess came back with our coffee. After a quick morning routine, we lounged in our room for a bit.

"Hey, I'm going to head out in a couple hours."

Jess looked up from the book she was reading. "Oh?"

"Yeah, Lucas wants me to go with him to talk to his mom. See if she knows anything about what he's going through."

She raised her eyebrows. "Sounds a little intense."

I huffed. "To say the least."

I decided to get ready early just for something to do. I spent the rest of the time losing myself in a painting of a cabin and some trees.

"Nice," Jess cooed.

I shrugged. "Meh. It's just keeping me busy."

"Well, it's beautiful."

I raised a brow. "You always say that."

She smiled. "I always think your stuff is great."

I mirrored her smile and grabbed my purse. "Lucas should be here in a few minutes."

"Text me later."

"Of course."

I sat on the stairs and stared out the window until I saw Lucas. I was worried about him driving but he seemed coherent.

"Does Kristoff know you borrowed his car?" I asked, climbing into the passenger's seat.

"You mean steal." He winked.

I shook my head with a snicker. "You're asking for it."

He chuckled. "He'll get over it."

Behind the wheel, Lucas was quiet. He stared at the road, seeming on autopilot.

"Your mom still at the hotel?"

"Huh?" He glanced at me. "Oh, yeah, she doesn't have a place here yet."

"Yet? So, she's moving here?"

"Hell, I don't know. She may go back to Portland. We haven't talked about it."

"I see."

"Don't worry. If she seems off, it's really not about you. She's just…"

"Just what?"

"Confused. My mother doesn't like The Order. She knows what they did was on them and only them."

"What about Katherine?"

"Katherine feels a little differently about them."

"She doesn't think they're good guys, does she?"

"Honestly, at the very least, everyone knows that they're corrupt. They also know there are some shady things going on, even if they don't realize they're pure evil."

"After what they did to you, she should know they're evil. Even if she does believe it's my fault. Why is that?"

"I don't know. It's crazy. That's all I've got."

I sighed. "I wish they'd just disappear."

He chuckled. "I've spent my entire life wishing that."

He fell silent again until we pulled up to the hotel. Margaret came outside to meet us. She pulled Lucas into a hug and unexpectedly, pulled me into one next. "It's so good to see you."

"Yeah," was all Lucas said.

We headed to Margaret's room on the second floor. She seemed to have something on her mind. Something in her eyes told me she had something to say.

"Should I wait in the car?" I whispered to Lucas.

His eyes bored into mine. "Why?"

I shrugged. "I don't know. I feel like she wants to say something but won't with me around."

He shook his head. "You're fine. Please stay."

I nodded and sat on the couch bedside Lucas.

"So," Margaret started, sitting in a chair across from us.

"What brings you here? I know you said you'd visit but I have a feeling there's a specific reason you're here."

Lucas pursed his lips. "There is, actually."

"What's on your mind?"

"This," Lucas said. He reached into his bookbag and handed her Rebekah's journal.

Margaret flipped through the pages and her face fell. "This," she murmured.

"Wait," Lucas said, "have you seen that before?"

"I have."

"What aren't you telling me?"

"Lucas…I wanted to protect you. Your brother too."

"That's great, Mother. Help by answering my question."

"I'm not fond of this new tone of yours …but you're right."

"About?

"That I'm keeping secrets."

"Tell me about the journal. Please."

She sighed and lowered her head before beginning. "This...condition. Is it happening to you or Kristoff?"

Lucas nodded. "Me."

Margaret sighed again breaking eye contact. "I found out that this—Rebekah was a relative of mine."

"We already knew that."

She tilted her head, confusion all over her face.

"Moe told us," he said.

"No, I mean she was a relative of *mine*, not your father's."

Lucas nodded.

"I never thought it could be hereditary until…" She broke off, still not making eye contact.

"Until what?" Lucas pressed.

"Until—it happened to me."

I felt Lucas squeeze my hand and the oxygen was sucked from my lungs.

Lucas spoke first. "What?"

"It happened to me."

"No, I—I heard you. I'm just…"

"Processing," I whispered.

He glanced at me. "Yeah."

She nodded, finally looking up.

"How did you stop it?" I asked.

"Yeah, that's kind of been the issue," Lucas said. "We don't know how to stop it. Mom, I—I hurt someone. I hurt someone seriously. He could have died. On top of that, I was a total jerk to Daisy, and the worst part is I don't even remember half of it. How do I make it stop?"

"I get it. It's like waking up after being drunk with only pieces that come back to you. And some that don't; maybe never will."

"So, what can we do?"

She looked away. "I don't know."

Lucas inhaled. "What the hell does that mean?"

"It means I don't know, Lucas. Don't you understand yet?"

"Understand what?"

Her voice rose. "This is why I left."

"Wait…this? As in this condition?"

"I couldn't be a good mother to you. I was unable to be a good wife, as well. I had to leave to protect the people I loved."

Lucas's voice cracked when he answered, "Then why now?"

I could hear the tears in his words and felt my own beginning to form.

"It just…stopped one day a couple of years ago. I don't know how or why."

"So, you're—cured?"

"I don't know if I would call it that, but I feel fine."

Lucas sighed before asking. "Why did you wait so long to come back?"

"I had to be sure that whatever had happened to me was gone for good."

"And?"

"And I believe it is, but I don't know why. And now that it's happening to you…"

"When did it stop?" I asked.

She moved her gaze to me. "I can't be sure, but I woke up one morning feeling—different. More myself. It was the summer before last. July, I think. I waited to make sure it was permanent."

"And Kristoff doesn't know this?" Lucas asked.

She shook her head.

"Mother—Kris is so angry. He's so hurt. If he knew why you truly left…"

"I know," she interrupted. "I thought not telling you would be better. I didn't abandon you. I would never abandon you."

"He needs to know that. More than I ever did."

She nodded. "I know. I'll tell him. I promise."

We headed back to the car, but Lucas sat without even turning on the car.

"Are you okay?"

He glanced at me and forced a smile. "I will be. It's a lot to take in."

"Yeah, tell me about it," I murmured.

"Daisy…what's going on with you?"

"What do you mean?"

"I know you. Something's up, besides me. If you think I can't handle it, you're wrong. Take your own advice and let me help."

"I just didn't want to put anything else on your plate."

He raised his eyebrows.

"Okay, don't say it. I get it."

Chapter 22

JESS CALLED *me the very next day. I didn't want to talk over the phone, so we met at the café again.*

"Any dreams?"

I shook my head. "Not last night, thankfully."

"I know these dreams scare the hell out of you, Dais, but in order to find out what's going on, you need to see him again."

"I know," I said, nodding. "I just wish I could confront him here—like, in the waking world."

"Waking world?" She smirked.

I waved her off. "You know what I mean."

"Do you know anything else about him?"

"Just that he saved me. I still don't know why."

"Well…wouldn't you?"

"If I saw a crash, yeah, I'd go help if I could, but you and I both know there is more to this than a simple random act of kindness."

She sighed. "Yeah, I do know that."

"So, either way, I have to find him. Somehow."

"I researched for hours last night, and I found exactly five pounds of

nothing. Nothing on dreams. At least, nothing on dreams like yours. I did find a lot of information about premonitions. I've read tons of articles."

Her eyes widened. "Like what?"

I hung my head. "Nothing that helps."

She sighed. "We'll figure it out."

"I hope so. I don't know how much more of this I can take."

"Until then…coffee?"

I forced a smile. "Got anything a little stronger?"

Jess giggled. "Actually—I might."

I raised my eyebrows. "I was only kidding, but now that you mention it…"

She laughed again and rose to her feet, offering me her hand. "Up."

"Now?"

"Why not?"

"It's barely noon."

"It's twelve fifteen."

"Point stands."

"Whatever. It's five fifteen somewhere. You in or not?"

I sighed but my smile hadn't faded. "In."

She squealed. "Yay! Let's go. I hope wine is okay. I kind of stole it from my mom. It was a couple weeks ago, and she didn't seem to notice so… I think we're safe."

"Rebel."

She giggled as I followed her out to the car. I let my mind wander just long enough for thoughts of the dreams to come back.

"You okay?"

I turned to Jess who glanced at me before turning her gaze back to the road.

I shrugged. "Yeah. Just thinking."

"Maybe you shouldn't think so much."

I chuckled. "Yeah, if only I could stop."

She pulled into her driveway. "Wine will help."

I followed her up to her room and turned away from her dresser. It was once lavender with flowers and birds. I helped her paint it when we were kids. I sighed.

"What is it?" Jess asked.

"Nothing. Just, everything."

We sat on the floor facing each other. "Here," she said, pulling out the wine.

I looked at it. The cork was half missing and torn apart. "Umm…"

"Yeah, I couldn't get it out."

"You can't pull it out," I said, laughing. "You need a corkscrew."

"I know that now."

I laughed again, shaking my head. "Should we check downstairs?"

Jess shook her head. "I already looked. I can't exactly ask my mom where she keeps it."

"Hand me your kit."

"My what?"

"Your manicure kit."

"Why?" She grumped.

I waved my hand at her. "Relax, and hand it over."

She reached into her bag and grabbed her kit.

"Don't break anything."

I rolled my eyes, digging through the bag until I found her manicure scissors."

"Whoa, what are you doing?"

"Would you chill, already?" I laughed. I took the scissors and used them to tear apart the cork until there was a big enough chunk missing I could pull it out. "See?"

Jess gave me a weird look. I handed her back the scissors. She stared at them for a second before putting them away.

"You're a nut," she said with a smile.

"You're the one without a corkscrew."

She chuckled. "Well, it's open so it's okay you're a nut."

I gave her a mock glare. "Okay, so what are we drinking to?"

"To…"

"Friendship," I said.

She singsonged, "Boring."

"Fine—to wine."

"Kind of on the nose, but I like it. Okay, to wine."

We laughed and it was a relief to feel normal again. I don't know what I would have done without Jess.

Chapter 23

HE DIDN'T SAY anything right away. He let me get it all out before saying a word.

"Daisy…"

"I know."

"All this time, and you said nothing?"

"Jess knows."

He nodded. "I'm glad for that but you shouldn't keep things like this from me. I understand why you didn't tell me but…"

"I can't risk stressing you out more. It seems that's what brings on your blackouts."

He sighed. "I've felt okay the past couple days, but I still feel different. Like there's something inside me trying to surface. I can control it for a while, but it eventually takes over. It's like being possessed."

"That sounds terrible."

"I just don't understand why my mom's blackouts just…stopped."

"Maybe yours will, too."

"When? I can't sit around waiting for a miracle. I could kill someone or throw all our secrets out into the world the next time it happens."

"I get your point." I leaned against him, and he automatically put his arm around me.

"We need to figure out how your mom got hers to go away."

"It all makes sense in a way," he murmured.

"What does?"

"Why she left. I know she didn't tell us because she's worried about The Order finding out. What they might do to her."

"The same way Rebekah was scared."

He nodded. "Exactly."

"We need more information. Has she told you anything else?"

He shook his head. "I haven't talked to her since yesterday."

"Okay. We need to go back and try to get to the bottom of it."

"Only after she talks to Kris. He's going to need some time to process. The investigation will have to wait a little while.

"That's perfectly understandable."

I flopped down on the bed and Jess looked up from her book.

"What's up?

I sighed. "Nothing. There's just so much going on."

"I don't want to stress you out anymore, but I have an idea."

I raised my eyebrows. "Shoot."

"Well, my mom has access to county files."

"Yeah…"

"If you want—whenever you're ready, of course—she could help you find your mom."

I nodded. "I don't think she wants to meet me."

"Why do you think that?"

"Because she gave me up. She gave *us* up."

"That doesn't mean she didn't love you. Maybe she was trying to give you a better life."

"Fat lot of good it did," I grumbled.

"You won't know until you try."

"I'm not ready for all that right now."

"I know. But keep it in mind if you decide you want to."

"I will. Thanks, Jess."

Exhausted, I decided to head to bed early but my head was so busy I couldn't quiet my thoughts enough to feel sleepy. I just kept replaying everything in my head, tossing and turning for hours before I finally dozed off.

When I opened my eyes, I knew I was dreaming. I was in a hotel lobby but not like the one where Margaret was staying. This one was bigger and more luxurious. Huge armchairs, fancy curtains, and floral carpeting. I stood up, feeling a sense of familiarity even though I had never been here before. A voice behind me pulled me from my thoughts.

"Miss?"

I turned around, and as soon as I saw him I knew something crazy was unfolding. I knew his eyes. Somehow. The big, round, dark eyes. Eyes like—like my dad's. The eyes I always found such comfort in when I was little. I didn't realize I even remembered my dad until I saw those eyes. I experienced flashes of him and a flood of memories: of dancing with him in the living room, of laughing at his funny faces at the dinner table. I shook my head to clear my mind, thinking my eyes were playing tricks on me, but when I looked at him again it was clear he was real. I squinted my eyes, staring at the boy. He was smiling like we were best friends.

"I'm sorry," I said, "do I…"

"Oh, how rude of me. I'm Bane," he held out his hand.

"Daisy." I took his hand, and he actually gave me a respectful grip instead of the tender grip of the fingers most men give me, like I'm made of glass.

"I know," he said.

"You…know?"

"Well…"

"Who are you?"

I knew the answer. I had to. I needed to hear him say it before I would let myself believe it.

"I—I believe I'm your brother."

As soon as I processed the words, I found myself awake with Jess staring at me.

"You okay?" She asked. "You seemed like you were having a nightmare."

"I'm not sure what just happened," I said, sitting up.

"Was it—one of those dreams."

I squinted my eyes. "No, I don't think so, but it definitely wasn't normal."

"What do you mean?"

Jess—I might have just met my brother."

"Wait—you mean met? As in…"

"I think he has what I have. I don't think it was just a dream. I think he was really there, and Jess—he looks *just* like my dad."

She opened her mouth to speak but nothing came out.

"I know what you're thinking. I never really remembered him, but seeing my brother—it's like it triggered some old memories. But it doesn't make sense. How can we have the same dad?"

"I don't need to explain *that* to you, do I?" she smirked.

"Jess, I'm serious. I've barely even come to terms with the fact my mom wasn't my mom. Now I find out my mom wasn't the only one my dad was with."

"Daisy, this doesn't mean infidelity. Sometimes people just don't stay together."

I nodded. "I hope that's all this is. But aside from that, he really was there. He knew who I was."

"That's *crazy*."

"I know. How can there be another person like me?"

"He's your brother, Daisy. It makes sense."

"I thought the accident is what gave me the abilities."

"Maybe they were there all along and just dormant. Maybe the accident triggered them."

"There are *way* too many maybes. I need answers."

She nodded. "We need to find your brother in the... waking world."

"Waking world?" I smirked at her.

"You're the one who called it that first."

"I know. I think I should look for where I saw him. See if it's a real place."

"Sounds like a plan. Let me fire up my laptop."

Chapter 24

JESS HANDED *me a glass of wine and set the bottle on the floor beside her.*

"No matter what happens, there's always wine," she said with a laugh.

"I wish that was all it took."

Her smile faded but she tried to hide it.

"You do believe me, don't you?" I asked.

"Of course, I believe you, but what exactly are you referring to?"

I shrugged. "I don't know. Everything? At least that he's real."

"The guy?"

I nodded. "My rescuer."

"You know what you saw."

"That's what I said, but the cops and doctors told me it was in my head, remember? That I imagined him. The head trauma confused me."

"Is that what you believe."

I sighed. "I'm not sure anymore."

"Well, I believe you. You were awake when you saw him, so you weren't dreaming, and I highly doubt you were having full blown halluci-

nations. Then he's appearing in your dreams after that. Even if you could argue his existence, you know the dream you had came true. You know that much. If we can believe that, we can believe in him."

I nodded. "You're right. He was real but he's nowhere to be found. Out here anyway."

She smirked. "The waking world."

"Exactly."

She raised her glass. "To the waking world."

I chuckled and tapped my glass against hers.

"I think we might be able to figure out what's going on."

"How?"

"Well, first thing's first if we want answers. You need to try and remember as much as possible. Any tiny detail might spark something you didn't even know you remember. A smell or a sound."

"How can I make myself remember—what I can't remember?"

"Well, let's try something. Close your eyes."

I narrowed my eyes. "Really?"

"Come on, trust me."

I sighed and closed my eyes.

"I want you to put yourself back there."

I immediately opened my eyes, shaking my head. "Jess, I can't do that."

"It's over, Dais. You're safe now. It's not going to happen again. I'm just asking you to remember. That's all."

I sighed again but closed my eyes, imagining myself in the road again. "Okay, I'm there."

"What do you see?"

"Nothing. I can't open my eyes."

"What do you hear?"

"A voice. A male voice."

"What's he saying?"

"He's asking me my name, but I can't answer. He's telling me I'm going to be okay."

"What happens next?"

"I open my eyes. I see a boy about my age. He looks—scared."

"Scared?"

"Scared for me. Worried. Like he knows me. I tell him my name. I close my eyes again, but before I do I notice yellow flowers near the curb, growing through cracks in the concrete."

"Flowers. That's good. Anything else?"

I shook my head. "No, I'm falling asleep. His voice is fading."

"What happened next?"

I opened my eyes. "I woke up in the hospital."

She inhaled and nodded.

"Nothing new."

"Well, you remember flowers."

"That's not significant."

"Maybe not, but it's a start. It means there's more in there."

"I think you're right about the dreams. I need to wait for another one. I need to wait until I see him again."

"Well...until then—wine."

I smiled. "Wine, it is."

She reached her glass towards mine again and bumped the bottle with her elbow sending it rolling onto the floor, soaking the carpet in red wine.

"Shit," she shouted.

I shot to my feet. "I'll get some towels."

Chapter 25

"I THINK the hotel is a real place," I said.

"I don't see why it wouldn't be. Do you know where it is?"

I closed my eyes trying to remember what I saw. "It was old-fashioned. I'm not sure if it was old but it had a classic feel. Very fancy."

"Hmm."

"I know. Not very helpful."

"Anything else?"

"There was stationary at a front office. I think it was one of the missions."

"Missions?"

"Yeah, like the buildings in an area meant to spread faith."

"Like a church."

I shrugged. "Not exactly. Sort of. Not important. I just know I saw the word 'mission.' Either mission something, or something mission."

"You said it was a hotel."

"It was. Maybe it was converted."

She leaned closer toward her laptop. "Well, what about this one?"

I moved beside her to see what she found. She clicked on the gallery.

"Wait…there. Click on the picture of the lobby."

The picture looked a bit different in black and white, but I recognized it immediately. The grand archway, the dome, towers and chandeliers. The tile entry led to a beautiful room adorned with large, floor-to-ceiling windows with flowing curtains and soft, oversized armchairs. It was like an old castle in the middle of a bustling city.

Other pictures revealed a beautiful, grand staircase with a huge fountain on the tiled floor below.

"Here?"

"Jess, that's it. That's what I saw."

"Okay then it actually *is* a hotel. It's called The Mission Inn."

I smiled. "Oh my god. We found it. I can't believe we found it. How did you do that?"

"Just searched old-fashioned hotels and missions. First page."

"Where is it?"

"Well, the good news is, it's in California."

"And the bad news?"

"It's still a bit far. Downtown Riverdale."

I furrowed my brow.

"Oh wait. Side. River*side*."

"I think I know where that is. It's not that far."

"Internet says about four and a half hours."

"Up for a road trip?"

She shot me a look. "Are you kidding me? My mom would flip."

"Jess, you're eighteen."

"Yeah but…"

"But what? Do you not want to go?"

"No, I do. I just don't want my mom to think I don't want to be here or something. I already don't really spend time with her."

"Well, how about this? Ask her and if she's okay with it, I'll help you plan an outing. Just the two of you."

She sighed. "Really?"

"Really."

Okay. Deal."

"It's going to be fun. A little intense, a little scary, for me anyway, but fun."

She smiled. "I'll go talk to her."

"Want me to come?"

"No, I don't want to put her on the spot."

I nodded. "Gotcha."

She headed downstairs and I started a new painting while I waited. She came back before I even started mixing the paint.

"Well?"

A very triumphant grin spread across her face.

"Yes?"

She squealed. "When can we leave?"

"Hold your horses. Geeze."

"Daisy, we've never been on a road trip together. We've never even left the city together."

"Well, it's not really a road trip. Maybe nine hours round trip."

She waved me off. "Whatever. Close enough."

"Then, we'll probably stay a night so we're rested for the drive home. Meaning, you should pack an overnight bag."

She smiled again and her eyes brightened.

"We can take turns driving," I jangled the keys.

"Daisy, you don't have a license."

"Not technically, but I was only forbidden to drive while I was healing to make sure I wouldn't have seizures or blackouts. Seeing no color was never really the issue."

She pursed her lips. "Just don't get pulled over."

"Not in the plan."

She ruffled through her closet, stuffing clothes into a duffel bag. I stifled a laugh. "Jess, we're going to be gone for one day. You don't need three different outfits."

"I want to be prepared for anything."

I rolled my eyes. "Yeah, yeah."

"Do you have any cash?"

"I haven't worked since the accident, but I still have a bit in the savings account my mom started for me. I can cover a hotel room for one night."

"Well…not at *that* hotel?"

I raised my brows. "No?"

"Hell no."

"I figured it's expensive, but…"

"Two hundred fifty per night, Daisy. And that's the lowest."

"Yikes."

"Exactly."

"Okay, I'll grab us a motel room then."

"Sounds good."

I helped her finish packing the essentials.

"We leave bright and early in the morning," I said.

She nodded. "Do you think he'll still be there?"

"I know he will. I feel like he's waiting for me."

It started like the last dream, in The Mission Inn's lobby. He was there beside me as if we had been there for hours.

"Is this real?" I murmured.

He smiled and again, I felt that eerie connection to my dad.

"It is real. You can do it, can't you?"

"How do you know that?"

"I know a lot of things, Daisy."

"I'm coming to meet you."

His smile returned. "I know."

"Will you be here?"

"I'm not going anywhere."

"You're…staying here?"

He shrugged. "Unofficially."

I furrowed my brow.

"Don't worry about it. I'll explain when you get here. You have to wake up first."

I opened my eyes to see the clock on my nightstand reading 5:42 am. I decided to let Jess sleep while I packed the car and woke her up at six thirty.

"Time to get up," I said, nudging her.

She groaned. "What time is it?"

"Time to leave."

She sat up but still had her eyes closed. "I need coffee."

"I already packed the car. We'll get coffee on the way."

Her eyes shot open. "You packed the car?"

I shrugged. "I was up."

"Thanks."

"Sure. Now, let's go. We have a long drive."

"Coffee on the way?"

I nodded. "Promise."

She finally got out of bed and stumbled into the bathroom like she was drunk.

Jess took the first shift driving, too worried I'd get us into trouble.

"You can drive when it gets dark."

"Jess, we're going to be there by ten a.m."

"Then…I guess I'm driving."

I rolled my eyes. "Fine. Just remember it was your idea."

"Did you text Lucas?" She asked.

I gasped. "Oh my god. I was so distracted…"

"He doesn't know?"

"I'll text him right now."

(Me) Hey, sorry I didn't tell you, it all happened so fast but I'm going to be out of town until tomorrow. Maybe longer."

(Lucas) What's going on?

(Me) It's a long story but I'm fine.

(Lucas) Where are you going? Are you alone?

(Me) Riverside. I'm with Jess. I won't be long. I'm meeting someone who might have some answers about my family. I promise I'll explain everything later.

(Lucas): Be safe and let me know when you get there.

(Me) I will. I love you.

(Lucas) Love you too. Please be safe.

Jess glanced at me again. "Lucas?"

"Yep. Thanks for reminding me. I didn't want him freaking out if he went looking for me and I wasn't there."

She nodded. "So we're set, right?"

"Yeah, we're good."

"Good." She pressed her foot a little harder on the pedal

with a huge smile on her face. Her smile started to fade after a couple hours, and we stopped for gas in Santa Barbera.

Jess groaned. "My foot is cramping like mad."

I laughed.

"Yeah, let me hear it."

"Hey, you're the one who wanted to drive."

"Yeah, yeah."

"I'll take over for a bit. Nothing's going to happen."

She nodded. "Fine. I'm gonna got grab some snacks and another cup of coffee."

"I'll be in the car."

Chapter 26

TAKING the coastal route was a good choice. The scenery was absolutely beautiful and a cool breeze danced across the water. We even rolled down the windows to smell the sea air.

"You were right," Jess said, slouching in her seat. "This *is* fun."

"See?" I agreed with her but couldn't deny my growing anxiety the closer we got to our destination. I wanted to know; I did. More than anything, I wanted answers. But I was also terrified of what I might find. There was already so much pain caused by my family's secrets. How much more could I take?

We stopped for gas again in Burbank and Jess decided to drive the rest of the way there. I almost dozed off when Jess pulled me out of it.

"Look," she said, excitement in her voice.

I opened my eyes, and she was pointing to a road sign that said *Pasadena 5 Miles.*

"Almost there," she added.

My anxiety instantly returned, and Jess clearly noticed. "Are you sure you want to do this?"

"What?"

"Daisy, if you don't want to do this, we don't have to."

"I do have to. I *have* to know the truth."

She sighed. "If there's anything I can do to help, just let me know."

"I'm glad you're here. That's all I need from you."

"I'll always be here."

I smiled. "I know. You're the best friend ever."

"Dam straight," she murmured.

I laughed and immediately felt better. I couldn't imagine doing this on my own. When Jess was with me, I felt like I could handle anything. She was always a little stronger and never had a problem lending me some of that strength when I needed it.

We entered Riverside and headed downtown toward the inn. It was huge, covering an entire city block. It was exactly like the pictures: pillars, domes, and towers like a castle. I smiled through the pressure in my chest.

"Are you ready?" Jess asked.

I inhaled, trying to stop shaking. "I may have had a bit too much coffee."

"It's just nerves, Dais. I've gotcha."

I grasped her hand, and we headed toward the entrance. I walked quickly, afraid that if I slowed down I'd never make it. We stepped inside and that dreamy sensation of the past flowed through me. Even though I had only seen it in dreams, I felt like I'd been there before.

"Doing okay?" Jess whispered.

I nodded. "I think so."

"Do you see him?"

I scanned the lobby. "No."

"Are you sure?"

"Yeah, he's not here right now."

"Should we wait?"

"I don't know. It's not like I can call him."

"Let's sit. If he knows you're coming to meet him, he'll show up eventually."

We plopped down in the soft armchairs. I listened to the chatter in the background, the low hum of voices and machines.

"Do you have a book or something?" Jess asked, grabbing a book from her bag.

I shook my head. "I'm okay."

"Want me to go ask someone?"

"Ask them what?"

"I don't know. Maybe he asked to be notified when you got here."

"I don't even remember what he told me his name was."

"You know yours."

I nodded. "Sure. I'll go."

I headed up the counter. The lady there was young and attractive with dark hair pulled back into a right bun.

"Can I help you?"

"My name is Daisy Carmichael. I think someone is waiting for me."

She pulled her eyebrows together in confusion. "A guest here?"

"Yes."

"Okay, what's their name?"

"Umm…I don't actually know."

"You don't know who you're meeting?"

"It's sort of a long story."

"I can't help you find a guest without a name."

"Yes, Ma'am. I'm asking if anyone has asked to be notified when I got here."

"One moment." She walked to another counter and typed something into a computer. I watched as she scanned the screen. "I don't see anything here. No notes that I can find."

I sighed. "Okay. Thank you."

"Is there anything else I can help you with?"

I shook my head. "No, it's okay. I'm going to wait in the lobby if that's okay."

"Of course. Let me know if you need any help."

I nodded and sat back down beside Jess.

"Anything?"

"No. I don't get it."

"Don't worry. He'll be here."

"Jess...what if..."

"What if what?"

"What it—they're just dreams."

"Like, regular dreams?"

I nodded.

"No way. No offense, Daisy, but you're not that lucky."

I laughed before I could stop myself. "Yeah. Ain't that the truth."

She smiled and handed me a book.

"What's this?"

"It's called a book. There are words inside."

I shot her a look.

"Just something to keep you entertained while you wait."

"Thanks."

I tried to read, but every time I got to the bottom of the page, I realized I had no idea what I just read. I closed the book and sighed.

"What's wrong?" Jess asked.

"I can't focus. I don't understand why he's not here."

"Just be patient."

I shook my head. "I think we've wasted a tank of gas on this one. A couple."

Jess sighed. "You usually know the difference, right? Between regular dreams and—irregular ones?"

I nodded. "Always."

"And these?"

"Felt real. Very real."

"So, he'll be here, Daisy. Have faith."

I glanced at my cell. 11:05. "Jess, it's been an hour."

She looked up from her book. "What do you want to do?"

"I don't know, but he isn't here."

She opened her mouth to speak but was interrupted by a voice behind me.

"If you're talking about me…"

I looked up to see him. My brother. He *was* real and he was there. I tried to say something but nothing came out. He was smiling like he was enjoying some private joke. I rose to my feet. "You're here."

"I am."

"We need—"

"To talk. I know."

Jess followed my lead and stood up staring like he was a ghost.

"Hi," he said, extending his hand. "Bane."

She hesitated a moment, looking at me before taking his hand. "Jess."

"So, are you—related?" Bane asked.

I answered first. "Not by blood, but I consider her my sister so anything you have to say to me, you can say to her."

He nodded. "Understood."

"Your name is Bane?"

"Bane Donovan."

"That's unique."

"My mother was a unique woman. My adoptive mother, I mean."

"Was?"

He pursed his lips. "She—passed. A while ago."

"Mine, too. I'm sorry."

He broke eye contact and cleared his throat. "We have a lot to talk about, but we need to go somewhere more private. Did you drive here?"

I nodded.

"Great, we can talk in your car."

He followed me and Jess to the car. Jess was silent, almost on autopilot. I wasn't sure what she was feeling, but it couldn't be any stranger than it was for me. I felt like I knew him, like I had always known him. We climbed into the backseat. I stared, waiting for him to start, but Jess broke the silence first.

"Were you really there?" she asked. "In Daisy's dreams?"

He nodded. "I was. I've known I could do it for a long time."

I had to ask. "How did you know about me?"

"My parents never hid the fact that I was adopted. I don't even remember when they told me. It was just something I knew from a very early age. When I turned thirteen and was starting to grow up, I wanted to meet my biological mom. Mary."

My eyes grew wide. "You met our mother?"

He nodded. "She told me about you. I always wanted a sister." He smiled.

I tried to smile back but wasn't sure if I had.

"I wanted to know why she gave me up. Why she gave *us* up."

"Did she tell you?"

"It's the usual story. She was young and wanted a better life for us than she could provide. She wanted us to stay together but it didn't happen that way."

"Why did you want to meet her?" Jess asked.

I shot her a look. "Jess…"

"No, it's okay," Bane answered. "It's a valid question. When I started having…dreams—I mean, when they started coming true—I wanted answers."

"So, they started when you were thirteen?" I asked.

"About. When did yours start?"

"Not until much later. Not until I was seventeen when I almost died in a car crash."

He gave me a confused look.

"Mine are also about…" I broke off, finding it painful to say out loud.

"About what?"

"People—people getting—hurt."

His eyebrows shot up. "What?"

"I save them."

He stared silently for a moment. "You *save* people? Like—literally?"

I nodded.

"That's—*amazing*."

"Really?"

"Yes, really. I would love to be able to do something like that."

Jess spoke next. "So, your dreams are different."

"Well yeah," he said. "They often come true, and I can dreamwalk, but I've never seen people dying or anything."

"Trust me, it doesn't feel like a blessing," I said. "I didn't ask for it. I also can't ignore it, or people die."

Bane shook his head. "Wow."

"They started shortly after the accident. The head trauma damaged my eyes. I don't see color, unless I'm asleep."

"Any idea why that is?" Jess added.

"I don't. So, you really can't see color? Like black and white?"

I nodded. "I can usually tell what color things are now, but I had to teach myself. It's not curable."

"I'm sorry."

"No, it's okay. It is what it is. I'm actually lucky. It could have been a lot worse."

"Well, I'm glad it wasn't. I'm happy to meet you."

"Why did you wait so long to find me?"

He broke eye contact for a moment. "I wasn't sure you knew—that you were adopted."

"I didn't."

"I was afraid of blowing up your life."

"There's more, though," I said. "Your face…your eyes…"

He nodded. "I know."

"Know what?"

"I know we have the same dad."

"David Carmichael was your dad too?"

"Yes."

"How did it happen?"

He shook his head. "I don't know. Honestly. From what I understand, our parents were together but very young. Teenagers. They both agreed to the adoption."

"But our dad…stayed with me."

"I heard."

"Did he know? That I was his?"

"I don't know. Why would he keep you but give me up?"

I shook my head. "Add that to the list of questions we don't have answers for."

Bane sighed. "There's something else you need to know."

I braced myself, knowing what he was about to say was something I probably didn't want to hear. Something that was going to change things again in some way. I inhaled, trying to stay calm.

"Our mother—Mary."

"Yeah?"

"She—also had…"

I felt my breath catch in my throat. I shouldn't have been surprised since it made perfect sense, yet I still felt a sense of shock.

"Dreams?" Jess asked.

He nodded. "Dreams. Visions. She told me she could dreamwalk."

Jess scoffed. "Dreamwalk?"

"That's what she called it."

"Like what we can do?" I asked.

"Exactly."

"So—it really was you. The dreams. You were really there."

He nodded. "Why else would I be here now?"

"Did Mary ever explain how or why she had visions?"

"She didn't. I don't think she understood it any better than we do. Some people are just—special. Different."

I tried to stifle the chuckle that escaped.

"What?" He mused.

Jess and I exchanged a smirk.

"Daisy has some—unusual friends," Jess said. "More so than either of you."

"It's kind of a long story," I added.

"Well—I'm not going anywhere."

"Oh," I paused, "I don't know if I should throw it at you right now. It's sort of…"

"Unbelievable," Jess said.

I nodded. "Exactly."

He perked up, interested. "Daisy, I can believe a lot."

"This is a lot more than a lot."

He smiled and leaned toward me. "Try me."

For a minute, he just stared at me. He stared hard like he was trying to read my mind.

"I told you," I said. "It sounds crazy."

"I'm still processing," he rubbed his forehead.

"It took Jess some time too."

"And you believe all this?" he asked, looking to her.

"I was there," she affirmed. "After what I've seen, I'd believe anything Daisy tells me."

"So, this…Lucas. He saved you?"

"Yes."

"And he wasn't supposed to?"

"Right. Well—he wasn't permitted to."

"By the evil covenant."

"The Order."

"Whatever. Do I have that right?"

I nodded.

"That's not even the part that has you questioning my sanity, is it?" I asked.

He stuttered a few times, trying to speak but not being able to find the words. He finally just raised his hands.

"I know," I said. "I read up on werewolf lore after Lucas explained it to me."

"And you've seen this?" Bane asked. "In person?"

"Yes."

He ran his hands through his sandy hair. "I don't know…I don't think… I mean, I believe you but…what the hell?"

Jess laughed. "Yeah, that was my reaction too."

"Geeze, Daisy. Your life."

"My life is a bit of a mess right now."

"Well, you have me now. We may not know each other yet but we're still family. I'd like to stick together if you'll have me."

I couldn't fight the smile that crept in. After losing my mom, family is all I wanted. "I think I can put up with you."

He chuckled. "You say that now."

Jess rolled her eyes. "Great."

"What?" Bane and I said is unison.

"That!" Jess retorted. "There are two of you."

Bane and I exchanged smiles. "She *is* my twin after all."

"September 23rd?" I asked.

"September 23rd."

Jess raised her eyebrows. "Again, I say—great."

"Aww, Jess. You know you love me."

She finally cracked a smile but rolled her eyes again.

Chapter 27

I STEPPED OUTSIDE, *feeling the warmth of the day approaching. I already knew where I was headed, but I didn't want to think about the dream. It was too horrific. If I didn't get there in time, it was sure to come true.*

The images kept replaying through my head, no matter how hard I tried not to think about them. The heat, the pain, the screams… All of it. I walked for at least thirty minutes until my legs started to ache, and I could feel blisters forming on the soles of my feet. I let myself fall to the ground on the curb in front of the house and waited. After ten minutes, I slowly walked to the door and knocked.

A young woman in her early thirties answered the door. "Yes?"

"I'm sorry to bother you, this might sound strange but, I think you have a gas leak."

"A gas leak?"

"Yes. In the back of your house."

She gave me a confused look and I knew I couldn't explain how I knew that. "My dog—got loose. I chased him into your backyard, and I smelled the gas."

Her already confused expression became even more apparent. I'm sorry for trespassing. I just needed to get my dog."

"So—where is he?"

"Who?"

"Your dog."

I pointed behind me. "Oh, he ran back towards my house." I felt like she knew I was lying but she stepped outside and headed toward the gate to her backyard. I followed. She stopped at what looked like the air conditioning unit. "Oh my god," she gasped. "You're right. This could have caused a fire."

The sounds of screams rang in my head, and I covered my ears as if that could stop it.

"Are you all right?"

I looked up, meeting her full chestnut eyes. "Yeah, I'm sorry. I'm fine."

"Well, thank you so much for letting me know about this."

I nodded and forced a smile.

"Are you sure you're all right?"

"I'm fine," I repeated.

She nodded without breaking eye contact. "Okay. Thanks again."

I stepped back through the gate without being asked and headed back towards home with the nightmare still on repeat. Sure, I could have waited and pulled her and her infant daughter from a burning house, but it made more sense to prevent it from happening at all. I stopped at the end of the street and watched the house to be sure I wouldn't still have to rush in. Sometimes events couldn't be changed and I could only save lives. Other times, they were a little more symbolic or abstract. Of course, I couldn't know why it was that way, but then again, I didn't know where they came from to begin with. When the repairman left the house a few hours later, I thought it was safe to return home. Hopefully, the dreams would stop for a while. Of course, I knew that was simply wishful thinking.

Chapter 28

"WHEN WERE you planning on heading home?" Bane asked.

"Tomorrow," I replied.

"I have a proposition for you."

I nodded. "Okay."

"Okay, so—we want answers, right? About our parents and why our dad kept you…whatever else."

"Right."

"Well—you know I've met Mary. I didn't ask for any details. I think I was afraid to know."

I nodded again. "I know what you mean. I've felt the same way since this all started."

"Do you feel differently now?"

"No, but I realize it doesn't matter whether I want to know or not, I need to."

"How do you feel about staying another day?"

"One more day?"

He nodded. "Mary is in Santa Monica. If we leave now,

we'd arrive around dinner time. I'd rather head over a little earlier in the day. Tomorrow."

I glanced at Jess who hadn't said anything in at least thirty minutes. "What do you think?"

She smirked. "And you gave me a hard time for packing extra clothes."

I rolled my eyes. "Okay, fine. You have I told you so rights. You in or not?"

Jess smiled. "I'm in."

"Great," Bane said. "I have a room here."

"You do?" Jess said.

"Well…sort of. Under the name Milo Montgomery."

"Who the hell is Milo Montgomery?" I asked.

"Well, for all intents and purposes, me."

"So—you lied?"

He shrugged. "I didn't lie, I fabricated the truth." He winked at me.

"Are you sure you can get away with that?" Jess asked. "I mean, it's technically fraud."

"This isn't my first rodeo," he said. "You have nothing to worry about, I promise. I'll take full responsibility if anything happens."

I smiled. "I definitely want to learn more about your life. About what led you to learn how to do something like that."

"My adoptive parents were really good people. But they also worked. A lot. I was often left on my own, fell in with the wrong crowd for a little while. You know? But I turned out okay in the end, and still have some illegal—yet highly useful —*skills*.

"Hmm."

Bane looked at Jess. "If you're okay sharing a bed with Daisy, I'll take the couch. I only have a single."

She nodded. "Sure. Not like we've never shared a bed before."

"Cool. Let's go. I'm on the fourth floor."

We headed to the elevator down the beautifully adorned hallway. The upstairs was just as fancily decorated as the lobby. I was almost afraid to touch anything for fear of ruining it.

"You hungry?" Bane asked.

"I am," Jess said.

"Jess is always hungry. We haven't eaten since this morning though; so yeah, I can eat."

"I'll have something sent up."

I reached into my bag to grab my wallet.

"Daisy, it's fine. Milo's got this, remember?"

I pursed my lips. "Shouldn't we at least pay for the room service? I mean—its already a risk…"

"Daisy, I promise you, it's all good. I'd never lie. Not to my *sister*."

"Nice," Jess said with a smile. "Very manipulative."

I chuckled. "Well, it worked. I trust you."

"Good."

Bane and I talked all night. Not about anything important or serious, which was a nice change of pace. Casual conversation was something I missed. We spent a lot of time laughing. We did talk about our childhoods but left our parents out of it, for the most part. His upbringing wasn't that different than mine, so we understood each other. It already felt like I had a brother—a real, true brother. It was better than I could have hoped.

The bed was so comfortable, I fell asleep only minutes

after lying down. No dreams disturbed me, thankfully. Jess woke me up at around eight the next morning.

"I made coffee," she handed me a mug.

"Thanks. Where's Bane?"

She pointed toward the bathroom. "Shower. Which means we can talk in private for a minute."

"What do you mean?"

She didn't answer.

"Jess, what?"

"It's probably nothing but…I'm not sure about him."

"About my brother?"

"Yeah, how do you even know he *is* your brother?"

"Because he's practically a clone of my dad, Jess."

She nodded. "Right. It's just…"

"What?"

"I don't know. Something just doesn't feel right."

"This is new to me too. I'm still processing things."

She waved her hand at me. "You know what? Never mind. I'm just being crazy. You're my best friend, and I guess I'm feeling a little territorial."

"Are you sure?"

"Yeah, don't worry about it. Forget I said anything."

I stared at her for a minute.

"Really, it's fine."

I decided to let it go. I knew there was something else she wanted to say, but I couldn't deal with anything else right now. Not after everything with my family. Jess was more like my sister so her getting along with Bane was important to me. I figured she just needed some time.

Jess and I got ready after Bane, and we headed out around nine thirty.

"Santa Monica, right?" I asked.

Bane nodded. "I'll be navigator."

He got into the backseat without having to be asked and Jess gave me a smile of approval. So far, so good.

"You're going to head back west," Bane said, "past Jurupa and Chino."

"Got it."

"You'll take the 60 to the 10."

I started the engine and drove west, my anxiety and uncertainty growing every mile we got closer. I inhaled, trying to focus on the road and not what lay ahead. Jess didn't ask if I was okay like she normally did. Bane, however, couldn't resist.

"Daisy?" He questioned.

"Did I miss a turn?"

"No, I just wanted to ask if you're doing okay. You seem —nervous."

I sighed. "I was trying to hide it."

"It's okay. I'm nervous too."

"So am I." Jess shrugged. "She's not even my mom and I feel a little uncomfortable. I'm sure it's a normal reaction."

I nodded. "I have so many questions. I'm trying to work out in my head which ones to ask first."

"I've been doing the same thing," Bane said.

"Any success?" I asked.

"Nope. You?"

I shook my head. "Nope. Maybe we can let her lead the conversation. See where it goes."

Bane sighed. "That's a good a plan as any at this point."

The rest of the drive was mostly silent with only a few navigation instructions from Bane. The traffic was light until we reached the 91. We ended up reaching Santa Monica by twelve thirty—later than originally planned.

"What's the address?" I asked.

Bane handed me a slip of paper.

"10th street," I murmured.

"Just up ahead."

I pulled up to the house with my entire body shaking. My stomach flip-flopped, and I froze.

"Daisy?" Jess whispered.

I turned to her but didn't answer.

"You don't have to do this."

"Yes, I do," I answered, nodding. "I'm just having a little trouble moving right now."

Bane got out first which helped me get out of the car. I stood at the end of the driveway but couldn't get any closer. The house was big but not a hilltop mansion by any means. It was clearly two stories with dormers and a balcony. It was modest but very well maintained. I envisioned Mary as a humble yet sophisticated woman. A woman who would serve tea. She would have a perfectly valid explanation for why she gave me up and would be thrilled to meet me. I shook the thoughts off, knowing that picturing her in any way would lead to disappointment. I already lost one mother; I had no idea how it would feel to lose another—even though I hadn't met het yet.

Jess gasped my hand. "It's okay, Daisy. You've got this."

I squeezed her hand in return, letting it bring me stability. I took a deep breath and headed up the driveway behind my brother.

"I'm not sure we should do this," I cautioned.

Bane shot me a look. "We came all this way."

"I know but—what if she doesn't want to meet me? Maybe we should have called first."

"I don't have her phone number, Daisy."

I sighed. "What if she'll be mad?"

"I guess we'll have to actually knock to find out."

I took a half step back when Bane knocked, resisting the urge to book it back to the car.

The door opened moments later, and the air was knocked from my lungs leaving my chest burning. She looked so familiar. I had seen her before. Every morning in the mirror. Long blonde hair and sky-blue eyes. Of course, she was older than me but the resemblance was eerie. I heard Jess mumble something and squeeze my hand again. Mary spoke before I could find the words.

"Oh my. You—must be Daisy."

I tried to smile but wasn't sure if I had.

"Nice to see you again, Bane."

"Sorry to drop by unannounced," he said .

"It's not a problem. Why don't you come in?"

I followed Bane into a spacious modern living room. A large couch and armchairs surrounded a modestly sized flat screen television with large bay windows on either side.

"Please, have a seat," Mary said, gesturing to the sofa. "I'm sure you have questions."

I still couldn't speak but so far, she was leading the conversation like I hoped.

"We do," Bane answered.

"Well, let me guess. This has something to do with your father, right?"

Bane and I made eye contact for a brief moment before looking back to Mary.

I nodded. "It does."

Chapter 29

MARY SIGHED. "I know you want to know about your father but there's no easy way to explain what happened.

"I can handle it," Bane said.

"After everything I've already learned recently, I know I can too," I added. I wasn't sure if that was true, but I didn't have any other words.

Mary nodded. "Daisy, has Bane told you about me? I mean about my—ability."

"The dreams?"

She nodded.

"Yes, he told me."

"Your father knew about the dreams. He knew about all of it."

"He knew?" I asked.

"He knew but it scared him. He seemed to be handling it fine for a while but..." she stopped and bowed her head.

"But what?" Bane pressed.

"When you and Daisy came along—when you were still young…"

"What?" Bane demanded. "Just say it."

"Bane, your visions and dreamwalking started a lot earlier than thirteen."

Bane's face fell and the color drained from his cheeks. "What?"

"I know you don't remember, but you were experiencing it before you were even able to talk. Once you were old enough, you tried to tell me and your father about it."

"I don't remember any of that," he said.

"Well, how could you? You were barely two. It scared your father so much he told you to stop talking about it. He claimed it was just your imagination."

"But it wasn't."

"No, but I think it made you ignore it for a while. At least until you were a teenager."

"Is that why he…left?" I asked.

Mary bowed her head again. "Yes. We were only eighteen-years-old and living with my parents. David just couldn't take it anymore. The abilities we had terrified him."

"So, he up and left?"

"Even with my parents help, I couldn't afford to give you the life you deserved. Your father knew nothing about your abilities, Daisy. When I put you up for adoption, I intended you to stay together. Your father loved you, Bane, but he didn't know how to deal with your dreams. I signed over custody of Daisy and made sure you went to a good family."

"That doesn't make sense," I said.

"Doesn't it? Your father had family money. When he left, he left me with nothing."

I had no idea what to say or how to say it.

"So, he knew Daisy was his?" Bane asked.

"Of course, he knew."

"You say he loved me but…he never came back for me."

"I know it seems cruel, but fear can make people do all sorts of crazy things. I'm sure he had every intention of telling you. I know he wanted to find you but…"

"He died," I said.

She nodded. "Yes."

"I didn't even realize I remembered him until I met Bane."

She gave me a confused expression.

"He looks just like Dad. It triggered some memories I didn't know I had."

"You didn't remember him?"

"Not really. I was really young when he passed. It took me years before I realized he wasn't coming back. I didn't understand death at the time."

"That must have been so hard," she said.

"I always felt like something was missing but didn't really grieve since I didn't remember much. Losing my mom…"

"Oh, god. Your mom? Daisy I'm so sorry."

"Thanks. It's been rough. Jess's mom took me in," I glanced at Jess. "She's been a lifeline for me."

Mary didn't ask me how she died, and I was grateful she didn't pry.

"You're very lucky to have a friend like her."

I forced a smile. I wanted to open up to Mary. Or I wanted to want to. I knew trusting her and feeling comfortable around her would take time, but I felt like I had already waited too long.

"So, he was going to come back for me?" Bane asked. "Really?"

"Yes. That was always the plan."

Bane glanced at me. "He never told Daisy about me."

"He was trying to keep her safe."

"From me?"

"From both of us. He didn't understand what we could do. He thought we were dangerous."

"Sometimes I feel the same way," I murmured. "Before the accident, my life was pretty normal. Now, everything is complicated. My parents are dead, I can't sleep without the fear of watching someone die, my best friend has been pulled into this mess, and my boyfriend's a…" I stopped immediately. Bane and Jess both looked at me wide-eyed. *Crap.*

"Daisy?" Mary asked. "Are you okay?"

"Uh, yeah," I replied. "I'm sorry, I'm fine,"

"I know the dreams can be scary and obviously not something we would choose."

"Do you have the same ones?"

She shook her head. "I often see things before they happen, but I've never seen someone—die."

"You're lucky," I groused.

"Maybe," she started, "but you get to save people. You make a difference."

I nodded. "I guess."

She moved on, possibly sensing my discomfort. "You said you have a boyfriend?"

"Umm, yeah."

"Tell me about him."

"His name is Lucas," I said.

"What's he like?"

He's a shapeshifter creature hell bent on taking over the evil secret organization that tried to kill us both, an organization to which his father and brother belong. He's also suffering from some genetic illness that's turning him into a violent jackass. On top of that, his long-lost mother just came back into the picture after turning into a bear and tearing apart one of the men who tortured her son. Any more questions?

"He's sweet," I said.

She realized she wasn't going to get anything more out of me and dropped the subject.

"What about you?" She asked, turning to Bane.

"Me?" he asked.

"Yeah, do you have a girlfriend? Or—boyfriend, maybe?"

"Oh, it'd be a girlfriend but I'm currently single."

"Just trying to get to know you a little better."

"Daisy is a really amazing painter," Jess chimed in.

She'd been so quiet, I almost forgot she was there.

"Is that right?" Mary asked. She sounded genuinely excited.

"Oh, well I don't know about amazing."

"You're too critical," Jess said. "Trust me, she's pretty amazing."

"It's funny you say that. I used to paint."

"Really?" I said.

"It's been a while since I've picked up a brush but it was one of my favorite things to do when I was younger."

"Maybe you should get back into it," I said.

"Maybe I should. I did love it."

I smiled. We had something in common already giving me a sense of hope. Maybe we could bond over our love for art. I still couldn't tell her about Lucas, no matter how badly I wanted to. I was lucky enough my brother didn't think I was a raving lunatic. I couldn't risk it a second time.

"Is something wrong?" Mary asked.

I shook my head.

"Nothing is wrong," Bane said.

"I have a feeling there's something you both want to say." She furrowed her brow, looking very hard into my eyes.

I shook my head again.

"I know we don't know each other very well but you can tell me anything."

I wanted to tell her about Lucas. About everything. I settled for a half truth. If she had visions too, she may have some advice.

"There is one thing," I said.

She smiled. "Shoot."

"It's going to sound completely crazy but—my boyfriend…" I paused, trying to find the words. "My boyfriend; he also has…dreams. Like ours."

Her eyes widened, and her eyebrows raised. "What?"

"I know. It's crazy."

"How…"

"I don't know. I thought at first that I was dreaming of him because he saved me. That's how it works for me too. The people I save often dream of me too. Like a connection I have with the people I'm meant to help."

"But—that's not the reason," she answered. "Is it?"

I raised my hands. "You know better than anyone, it isn't."

"Just— What are the odds? So, he saved you?"

I nodded. "He pulled me from my car. He called for help."

"Wow. And that's not the only time he dreamed of someone…"

"Dying?" I shook my head. "No."

"That *is* crazy."

"You believe me though, right?" I prodded.

"I didn't mean it like that. Of course, I believe you. It's just wild."

You don't know the half of it.

I inhaled trying to muster up the courage to say a little more. "Can I ask you something?"

"Anything," Mary answered.

"Do you know anything about—like—conditions common among people with our…abilities?"

"Conditions?" She questioned. "Like what?"

"It's not important," I evaded. "Never mind."

"Daisy, talk to me," she said, soothingly. "You can tell me anything."

I wish that were true. "It's just—my boyfriend."

She nodded, waiting.

"He's having a really hard time."

"How so?"

"I'm not really sure. He's acting different. Off. And usually remembers nothing."

"He's forgetting things?"

"It's more than that. It's like he completely blacks out, acts like a total lunatic, then wakes up the next morning seeming like himself again. He's not just forgetting things. He doesn't even know he's doing them. He's losing time. Huge chunks of time."

Mary nodded, slowly. "Actually—I might know something about that."

I froze, a nervous feeling brewing in the pit of my stomach. "What?"

"Daisy—your boyfriend—I know what he is."

For a moment I just stared, not even sure I was still breathing. Bane and Jess looked almost as distressed. If she really knew what Lucas was, if she even knew they existed, she might be able to help. However, if I misinterpreted what she meant, I could end up spilling more than I wanted. I thought it was best to play dumb first.

"What are you talking about?" I said, trying to force the emotion from my voice.

"Daisy, it's okay."

I shrugged. "What do you mean?"

She held up a finger. "Hang on. Let me show you something."

She got up from the couch and headed to the shelves beside the door. She shuffled through some old papers and retuned with a leatherbound book.

"What is that?"

"This is something I've had for many years. It was given to me by my grandmother. Your great-grandmother."

She opened the book. *The Therian Curses and Secret Orders.*

"I looked for years for something that could tell me why I was having these dreams..." Mary continued. "Until my grandmother gave me this book."

"I searched myself," Jess said. "Daisy and I both did. We never found anything like that."

"This book is—different."

"Different how?" I asked.

"Well, it's not published. It's self-printed and, as far as I know, the only one is existence."

Bane looked at me, confusion etched on his face.

"What does it say?"

"Much of it is not relevant but there are many pages that mention Therianthropy."

"Therian—what?" Bane sputtered.

"Theriananthropy. Have you ever heard of lycanthropy?"

"Werewolves," Jess murmured.

"Exactly. The therianthropes are slightly different. Legend says they can shift into many different animals. Some are limited to only one type, or a few types. Some can only change at night, and some are more—advanced."

"Advanced?"

She nodded. "Some have more potent abilities. Many call it magic but it's not mystical. It's just—science."

I pursed my lips giving her the most unreadable expression I could muster.

"I know it sounds like a bunch of crap but it's true. Like our visions. They don't make a lot of sense to us, but I believe the universe works in ways we don't always understand. That doesn't make it mystical. The universe has energy. Some special people—or creatures—are able to harness that energy and do incredible things with it."

"Like curses," I said.

Mary's face fell. "Like curses."

Bane's mouth dropped open and I could hear Jess audibly inhale. *Could this be true?*

"Lucas is…" I tried to say it, but it wouldn't come out.

"A therianthrope," Mary said it for me.

I nodded. "What do you know?"

She sighed. "I know that people like us, our entire bloodline are not meant to be. Something in the fabric of the universe got a little—torn."

"A flaw in the pattern," I said.

She cocked her head. "Exactly. How did you…"

"I've heard it before."

"A flaw in the pattern. Human beings are rarely meant to have these abilities. They're exclusive to the therianthrope."

"So, what does that mean for us?" Bane asked.

"It means Daisy made a possibly fatal mistake."

"What?" I shouted.

"Daisy—if they knew what you could do—what *we* can do, they won't stand for it."

"Lucas isn't like that."

"I know you think that because you like him…"

"Love him," I interrupted. "I love him. We love each other. He saved my life; he's always protected me…"

"Always?"

I fell silent, kicking myself for saying too much.

"Oh my god," Mary whispered. "He knows."

I didn't respond. Nobody did.

Her voice swelled. "He knows, doesn't he?"

I still couldn't say anything.

"Do you have any idea what that means?"

"Yes," I retorted immediately. "I do."

"Really…"

"Yes. Look, I know we're not considered safe to the—therian-whatevers, but Lucas is different. He knows what we can do, and he won't let anything happen to us. But something is happening to him. The same thing that happened to his mother."

"His mother?" Mary questioned. "Is she…"

"Dead?"

Mary nodded.

"No," I answered. "She's not dead. Whatever was happening to her just—stopped. She doesn't know why."

"Wait—that doesn't make sense," she said. "I know what this is. This curse."

"How?" I asked.

"It's in the book. Here."

She turned to a page halfway through.

"It says here that the condition consists of lost time, blackouts, confusion, personality changes, aggression and depression."

"Sounds about right," I said.

"Right, but it also says…"

"What?" I leaned forward to look at the page.

Victims of this curse may experience the condition for months and sometimes even years but eventually the disease proves fatal. There is no known cure at this time.

I choked on my breath. *Fatal?* "But…"

"His mother," Mary said.

"So, the book is wrong," Bane added.

Mary sighed. "Clearly, but…"

"But we still need to know how to stop it," I said. "If the condition is fatal and can last for an undetermined amount of time…Lucas…"

"Daisy, I might have an idea," Jess said.

"Anything," I answered.

"I was just thinking about what you were all saying about you being a flaw in the pattern. You're special, right?"

"Right."

She straightened before continuing. "Right, so if something is happening to Lucas. A therian-whatever, couldn't that have something to do with you?"

"Wait, what?" I spat. "You think I'm doing this to him?"

"No, no. Not like that. I mean, there may be a connection. Didn't you say that Lucas's mom had the same condition and it just cleared up out of the blue?"

I nodded.

"Daisy—when did you have your accident?"

I froze and pieces started clicking together in my head. Fitting like a jigsaw puzzle. "Oh. My. *God.*"

"Call Lucas," Jess ordered. "Now."

Chapter 30

I GRABBED my phone to call Lucas, who answered after half a ring.

"Daisy, what's wrong? Are you okay?"

"Lucas, relax, I'm fine. Are you?"

He hesitated before replying. "That depends."

"On?"

"Well—Kris says nothing happened, but I sort of…"

I prodded, "Sort of what, Lucas?"

"It's not a big thing, but I sort of—lost most of last night."

I sighed. "Again?"

"But Kristoff swore I didn't do anything weird. Except, I didn't do much of anything at all."

"Meaning what exactly?"

"I don't really know. I don't remember, but Kris said I was checked out. Like a zombie."

"That's—new."

"It's strange. I know."

I cleared my throat. "Lucas, I need to ask you something."

"What's going on?"

"I'll explain everything later but right now, I need you to tell me something."

"Okay."

"When did your mom's symptoms clear up?"

He sighed. "I don't know, Daisy. She said July but she doesn't know what day."

"You need to ask her again. You need to make her remember."

"Daisy, why? What is going on?!"

"I can't tell you."

"That's not gonna work for me, Dais. You need to talk to me."

"Look—I have to go. Please talk to her. I'll explain everything. I promise."

"Fine, but you'd better explain this soon."

"I will."

I hung up and turned to Jess. "We have to get home," I said.

Bane and Mary exchanged a look but didn't argue.

I'll be back," I added. "I promise, but Lucas needs me. I think I might know how to save him."

"Wait," Mary said. "Tell me what you figured out. I'd like to help if you'll let me."

"I don't know if you can."

"You don't know I *can't*," she said with a smile.

"Me too," Bane agreed. "We're family. Let us help."

I nodded. "Okay, look—my accident is what triggered my dreams, right? It's when all of this started for me."

Mary nodded.

"And Lucas's mom got sick years ago but her symptoms stopped. Two years ago. In July."

Bane's eyes grew wide. "Your dreams…"

"It's connected," I said. "Yes."

"If his mother got sick years ago, Lucas has time," Bane said.

"Maybe, but it's affecting him in ways that scare the hell out of me. If he doesn't hurt or kill someone, he could hurt or kill himself or expose his kind. If The Order finds out about this, he's dead. Do you understand that? They will kill him. We can't wait!"

Mary stilled. Staring at me. "What did you just say?"

Crap! "We can't wait…?"

"The Order? You know about The Order?"

"*You* know about The Order?"

Bane sighed. "This is gonna be a long day," he mumbled.

We were stopped for gas when my phone rang.

"Lucas?"

"Hey, I talked to my mom."

"What did she say?"

"Like I said, she doesn't remember exactly but she knows it was shortly after Independence Day. She remembered hearing fireworks about a week before."

My accident happened July 13th. It tracked.

"What does that mean?" he asked.

"I'm not sure."

"Then why did you need to know?"

"I'm on my way home and I'll explain it all. See you in a few hours."

He sighed. "Fine, but just so you know, not telling me has me really on edge. That's not the best thing for me right now."

"Just hold on for a few more hours. This is in person news. I might know how to help you."

"Wait, really?"

"I don't know yet, but maybe. I'll see you soon and we'll figure it out."

"Okay, call me when you're close."

"Promise."

I hung up and everyone was staring at me.

"Everything okay?" Jess asked.

"Fine," I answered. "He's just worried about me."

"I think you're killing him with suspense," Bane said with a laugh.

"He'll get over it," I replied. "Just a few more hours."

Bane took over driving, but Jess let me have the front seat. She always said she wasn't going to sit in the back of her own car, but I think she felt bad for me or something.

When we finally pulled up to Jess's house, we saw her mom's car.

"Your mom is home," I said. "That's going to be awkward."

She hesitated. "Okay, I'll go in real fast, make sure she knows I'm safe and I'll meet you back here so we can all talk to Lucas together. You should call him to tell him we're all coming over."

"Sounds like a plan." I texted Lucas.

(Me) I'm on my way to your place with Jess. I'm bringing guests but you'll understand when we get there.

(Lucas) Fine. Please hurry.

We waited for Jess in the car but none of us knew what to say.

"Does Lucas live close by?" Mary asked.

"It's Cayucos," I said. "Everything is close by."

Jess came sprinting back to the car in a different top.

"You changed?"

"I was all roadtrippy," she said.

"We all are," Bane added.

"We can all rest later. Let's go."

We headed over to Lucas's house. He was sitting on the porch when we pulled up. I got out first followed by Jess. Bane and Mary had a bit more difficulty. I'm sure they felt similar to how I felt meeting them.

"It's okay," I reassured them. "Remember, he's not like The Order."

Mary nodded.

Lucas pulled me into a tight hug.

"I missed you too," I said.

He moved aside and saw Mary. A look of recognition flickered across his face. "Oh my…"

"Lucas, this is Mary. She's my…"

"Mother," Lucas said, unable to hide the shock in his voice.

"And this is Bane. My brother."

Lucas smiled and went to shake Bane's hand.

"This is what you couldn't tell me?" Lucas asked. "You couldn't tell me you were meeting your family?"

"I wasn't sure how it was going to go. I didn't know what to expect."

"And?"

"Well, they're here so…

"It's really nice to meet you," Mary said, but I could hear her voice quake.

"We've heard a lot about you," Bane added.

"All good, I hope."

Bane grinned. "Not bad."

"I'm sorry about my initial reaction," Lucas said, looking to Mary. "It's just—she looks just like you."

Mary smiled. "I knew it was her the second I saw her."

"I do want to chat with you all, but I know something important is going on."

"Right," I said. "The reason we're all here."

Chapter 31

LUCAS STARED IN SILENCE.

"Are you okay?" I asked.

"I'm—working on it."

"There's one more thing," I said.

"What more could there possibly be?"

"Remember I asked about your mom?"

"Oh, right," he said. "I actually forgot about that."

"Lucas—my accident, the one that triggered my visions…"

"Yeah?"

"It happened July 13th."

He froze for a moment. "About a week after Independence Day."

"Exactly."

"Oh my god," he murmured. "Does this mean…what *does* this mean?"

I shook my head. "We're not entirely sure but it *has* to be connected."

"You're not the only one," Lucas said. "It's a bloodline. Your entire ancestry is a flaw in the pattern."

I nodded.

"Maybe not," Bane said.

"What do you mean?" I asked.

"Maybe we're not a flaw at all. Think about it. The universe has a design. If we weren't meant to be here, we wouldn't be."

"I think he's right," Jess said. "I never saw what you could do as anything other than a miracle."

I smiled.

"Maybe so," Lucas said, "but still, humans with these abilities are definitely something The Order wouldn't stand for."

Mary stiffened.

"Which is why they can't find out," he added.

Mary sighed and I finally had to say something. "I promise it's okay. Lucas will make sure nothing happens to any of us."

She nodded but didn't look convinced.

"I'm not your enemy," Lucas said. "I'm not like the evil bastards who run The Order."

"We have to understand what's happening to you," I paused and then blurted, "There *is* something Mary found."

Lucas raised his eyebrows.

Mary turned to Lucas but didn't make eye contact. "My family knew about—your kind."

"My kind?"

She nodded. "The therianthropes. Shapeshifters."

"How?" Lucas asked.

"I'm not sure. It's in an old book my grandmother gave me. I never thought to ask how she knew."

"What about what's happening to me?"

"There was something about that too. I think it's a curse."

Lucas stiffened, waiting for someone to explain.

"This Order," Mary started, "are they…"

"They're corrupt," Lucas rubbed the back of his neck, "but they didn't used to be. They used to be good. They helped keep our kind secret. They kept us safe. After I came along, they used my dreams to decide who lived and died. They said they were keeping the balance but it's not true. They just want power."

"Can they be stopped?"

Lucas scoffed. "I'm not sure. After all these years, I don't have a lot of hope for that."

"I guess we can deal with that later," I said. "We need to focus on getting you better."

Lucas nodded. "I think it's getting worse. Kristoff practically has me on lockdown. If The Order finds out, it's not just my life. It's his too. He knows about it, so he's complicit."

"What are you gonna do?"

"I need to talk to Moe," he answered. "And as much as I don't want to, I need to fill my brother in on everything that's happening."

I nodded. "Okay."

"I need to do this alone, but I'll keep you in the loop."

"I think we'll stick around," Bane said. "I'll get a hotel in town if that's okay."

I nodded. "Yeah, I'd like for you to stay until we figure this out."

Mary nodded. "Let us know if you find anything."

After dropping off Bane and Mary at a hotel, we headed home. The drive was silent. Neither of us knew what to say. It was all too crazy. If Lucas could be saved, we would do whatever was necessary.

"I hate waiting," I complained, stepping into our room.

"How are you holding up besides that?"

I shook my head. "I don't really know. My mom seems great, but I'm not buying that she doesn't know where that book came from."

"And your brother?"

Brother. "I love the fact that I have one. He also seems great, and we seem to get each other. It's just going to take some time for us to bond."

Jess nodded. "I feel like they're hiding something."

"Right? I feel the same way."

"Aren't you worried?"

I shrugged. "I don't know. I don't want to be. I want to believe I can have the family I always wanted. I loved my parents more than anything, but they're gone now. Mary and Bane are all that's left."

"You'll always have me," she said.

I realized then how everything I said must sound to her. "You'll always be my sister. Nothing will ever change that, and you cannot be replaced."

She smiled. "Maybe I felt a little threatened."

"There's no need. Having a brother is great, but you're my Jess. One of a kind."

"Damn straight," she murmured.

"So, what do you think about this whole curse thing?" I asked.

Jess shrugged. "It makes sense."

"I guess it does, but who would do something like this?"

"And why?"

"Actually, that's a better question," I acknowledged. "Why?

"The Order would kill him if they find out but—who other than The Order are strong enough to pull something like this off?"

I froze. "Oh my god!"

"What?"

"You're right."

"About?"

"The Order. They're behind this. They have to be."

"That doesn't make sense."

"Think about it," I urged. "All the trouble Lucas and I have caused and then Margaret rips apart Mr. White… It all makes perfect sense."

"Wait—they're trying to…"

"Get rid of Lucas," I finished her sentence. "They're threatened by him."

I grabbed my phone and texted Lucas.

(Me) Lucas, be careful what you tell your family. We think The Order is behind this.

(Lucas) Daisy, it's okay. I didn't want to scare you anymore than you already were, but this isn't news to me.

"He already knew," I said.

Jess exhaled. "Wow."

(Me) Okay. Call me when you have news.

(Lucas) I will.

• • •

I flopped down on the bed. "Back to waiting."

Evening came without any word. I wanted to call Lucas again, but I couldn't. I didn't want to pressure him. I knew I wasn't going to sleep with this eating away at my mind, so I downed a few shots of cough syrup before heading to bed.

"I don't know *how* you can do that," Jess said with a chuckle.

I shrugged. "It helps me sleep."

"Yeah, but it tastes *terrible*."

"Says the girl who drinks whiskey straight out of the bottle."

She burst into high pitched laughter. "I did that once."

I laughed, too. "My point stands."

She waved me off. "Whatever, crazy girl."

"I've missed that," I said.

"Miss what?"

"Laughing."

"Yeah—it's been a while, hasn't it?"

"Everything seems so…heavy all the time. It's nice to feel light for once."

"I know what you mean."

I got ready for bed, even though it was barely nine o'clock. I couldn't stand sitting around, distracted, waiting for my phone to ring. I pulled the easel with my newest painting into the corner of the room.

"You going to sleep?" Jess asked.

"I'm gonna try."

As soon as I could feel sleep coming on, I knew I was about to dream. I tried to fight it, but it was no use.

It was hazy at first and muffled voices echoed through the air. I waited a moment and the image cleared. I could see

Lucas. He was with Kristoff and Moe. I couldn't understand their words at first, until I heard my name.

"Daisy, if you can hear this, don't tell anyone," It was Kristoff. He was talking to me, but his lips hadn't moved.

"I know you're scared but this is all about you. Your entire bloodline. This has always been about you. It's why Lucas wasn't supposed to save your life. You're the key to everything. Please be patient and we will come to you as soon as we can. I'm going to find out how The Order is doing this, and I *will* stop them. I promise."

I wanted to reply but nothing came out. The vision began to fade. *No, not yet.*

I strained to stay with them, strained to keep myself grounded, but I was drifting into another place.

I was at the beach. The sun was setting, the sky was gray, and rain clouds rested across the horizon. The sand was cool against my bare feet. I was in my body this time. I glided toward the shore, reveling in silky softness caressing my skin. I wore the white nightgown my mom gave me before she passed, but I hadn't been wearing it when I went to sleep. I walked farther through the sand until the water brushed across my feet. I could hear the crashing of the waves in the distance and the cawing seagulls. I closed my eyes, savoring the serenity.

A loud sound pulled me from my thoughts. My eyes sprang open at the sound of a scream. *Oh no.*

Without thinking, I rushed into the water following the cries of help from the distance. I had no idea what I was heading towards. For all I knew I was swimming straight into a shark attack, but I didn't care. I kept going. The water was frigid, chilling me to the bone and making it difficult to keep moving. I felt as if I was going to freeze solid before I got to the person in need. I pushed with every ounce of strength I could muster.

I saw him, a kid. He couldn't be more than twelve. He was waving his arms as the waves broke over his head one after another. I swam his direction, but the current was too strong, pulling me towards the rocks. I realized I was in a rip tide and swam parallel to the shoreline until I no longer felt its pull. Then I turned and swam towards the boy.

I wrapped my arms around his waist. "Hold onto me," I said. "Keep your head up."

I swam at an angle, away from the undertow and toward the shore. When we were able to stand, I set the boy on his feet.

"Are you okay?" I asked.

He nodded, shivering from the cold. "You saved my life."

"Don't mention it. What were you doing out here with the conditions like this?"

He shrugged. "Best time to be in the water is when they tell you it's dangerous. You can only catch the best waves when the weather gets bad."

"Next time, listen; and stay out of the water when a storm is brewing."

He opened his mouth to reply but it was too late. I awoke to the sound of my cell phone ringing.

Chapter 32

I SHOT UP IN A PANIC.

"Lucas?"

"Daisy, it's Kristoff," he said, panic in his voice. "You need to get here. Now."

"What's going on? Is Lucas okay?"

"No. He isn't. Get here."

I shook Jess awake.

"What?" She groaned.

"I need to get to Lucas. Something is wrong. I just need your car."

"Wait," she said, sitting up. "I'll drive you."

"Thanks."

She rushed into the bathroom and came back out less than fifteen minutes later. "You had a dream, didn't you?"

I knitted my eyebrows in confusion.

"Yeah," she said, grabbing her sweater off the back of the chair. "I know you. Come on."

I followed her out to the car. "I did have a dream, but

Kristoff called and told me to come over," I said. "The dream is unrelated."

She nodded. "You never catch a break, do you?"

"Jess…it's Lucas."

"What do you mean?"

I shook my head. "Kristoff sounded terrified; and when I asked him if Lucas was okay, he said no."

"What the hell does that mean?"

I cupped my head. "I don't know. I didn't ask. I was afraid of the answer. What if…"

"Don't," Jess retorted. "Lucas is alive. If he wasn't, Kristoff would be at the door to tell you in person."

I nodded. "You're right."

"Try to stay calm. You'll figure it out, whatever it is."

I sighed. "Should I call Bane? Mary maybe? I said I'd keep them informed."

She hesitated. "Why don't you see what's going on first?"

"Yeah, that's probably a good idea."

Jess sped down the road like we were running from someone. I didn't complain. It was urgent. We pulled up to the driveway and I hopped out of the Honda before it stopped moving.

"Call me if you need me to pick you up," she called.

I nodded and ran up to the porch, but Kristoff opened the door before I knocked.

"Hey," I said. "What happened?"

Kristoff was disheveled and looked like he'd been crying. I'd never seen him like that before. His blonde hair was loose and tousled, and his light eyes were surrounded in dark circles.

"I don't know," he said. I could hear the pain in his voice. He *had* been crying.

"Okay, you're scaring me," I said.

He grasped my wrist. "Come inside."

He led me down the hall to Lucas's bedroom.

"All last night, I couldn't get him to say a word. Did you… hear me?"

"Last night? That was real?"

He nodded. "It was the only way I could talk to you and know for sure nobody else could hear me. I told you, you are the key to everything, and I meant it but I'm just not sure how. Lucas is—practically catatonic. He hasn't spoken a word since yesterday. I don't understand why."

I tentatively reached for the handle on the bedroom door. When I opened it, Lucas was lying in bed. His eyes were open, but he didn't stir at my intrusion.

"Lucas?" I said, kneeling beside the bed. He didn't respond, didn't even blink. "Lucas, it's Daisy. Can you hear me?"

Nothing.

"I don't understand," I said, turning towards Kristoff. "He looks perfectly fine."

"I know. He's been like this since yesterday. I couldn't even get him to eat or drink any water. Daisy, I'm scared. If this is what happened to my mother…"

"Kristoff, your mother was sick for years and she survived. This—is progressing much faster than that."

He nodded. "I know. And I *know* The Order is behind this. Moe and I are going to figure this out but, Daisy…"

"What?"

"Lucas is running out of time."

I sighed. "Let me call my brother. He and my mom can help. They know more than they are letting on."

"We're going to need to talk about that later, by the way," he said, "Your mom shouldn't even know we exist."

"I swear I didn't tell her."

"I know. Something very strange is going on."

I nodded. "Noted."

I left the room and walked back into the kitchen.

"Wait," Kristoff said.

"What is it?"

"Just—be careful what you say over the phone. I can't be sure of what The Order may or may not be doing."

"You got it."

Bane picked up after one ring.

"Hey, Daisy. What's going on?"

"I need you to meet me at Lucas's house."

"Now?"

"Can you get here? Or do you need a ride?"

"Umm, no, I'll order an Uber. See you in a bit."

"Please hurry, it's important. Oh, and Bane?"

"Yeah?"

"Bring the book."

"Got it. On my way."

I slumped down in my chair at the kitchen table.

"I called Moe, too," Kristoff said.

I nodded. "Is he coming here?"

"Soon. We're going to head to HQ and see if we can figure out what The Order is hiding. Whatever is going on isn't permitted."

"Meaning what?"

"The Order uses Lucas's dreams to make decisions about life and death."

"I know this."

"Right, so why would they want him dead?"

"I see your point."

"That means that the person, or people, doing this are not

doing it—legally. The Order won't stand for it. He's the son of an elder and the brother of a respected member. This will not end well for the people responsible."

I nodded. "They'll be…"

"Taken care of," he interrupted. "Yes."

"Meeting them in another mausoleum?"

Kristoff laughed. "No."

"I wasn't joking."

"The Order sets up gatherings like that, so people don't notice them. Headquarters is somewhere else."

"Where?"

He raised his eyebrows. "Daisy, do you really think I can tell you that?"

"Oh…right. Sorry."

A knock at the door had me instantly on my feet.

"It's Moe," Kristoff said.

I sat back down with a sigh. Moe walked in dressed in a dark gray suit, almost the same color as his hair, which was pulled back in a low ponytail.

"Hello, Daisy."

"Hi." It was all I could say.

"She knows what's going on and knows some people who might be able to help."

Moe nodded. "Who are these—people?"

"My—family," I said.

Moe glanced at Kristoff and back at me.

"It's kind of a long story," I said.

"I have time," Moe answered.

"It's okay," Kristoff said. "You can tell him."

I sighed. "Okay."

By the time I finished telling him everything, I saw the car pull up outside.

"They're here."

"We're not done yet," Moe said. "You do know I'll have to find out how your biological mother knows about us."

I nodded. "I know."

"For now, let's keep the focus on Lucas," Kristoff said. "He's fading."

Bane nodded. "We might know some things."

"Things we don't?" Moe asked.

Mary swallowed, looking more and more anxious. "My grandmother had this." She reached into her bag and revealed the book. "I'm not sure how much of it is true and how much of it is my grandmother's superstitions. She was—eccentric."

Moe reached for it. "May I?"

"Umm—sure," Mary handed him the book. "It's the only one in print."

"I'll be careful."

Kristoff moved in closer to his father as they browsed through the pages.

"Wait," Moe said. "Here. It mentions The Order."

Kristoff's jaw dropped. He instantly looked at Mary, thinking she might answer his question without having to ask. He was right.

"I don't know," she stammered. "I swear. However, my grandmother learned of these things wasn't shared with me. The book is all I have."

Moe looked at her with that same suspicion then turned back to the book.

"Therianthrope?" Kristoff mumbled.

Moe shrugged. "I've heard it before."

"I don't like it."

"It's more accurate than lycanthrope."

Kristoff laughed, which threw me off guard. "What, we're werewolves now?"

Moe smiled. "They used to think that."

Their voices were low like they were having a very private conversation which made all of us visibly uncomfortable and unsure how to act.

"There's nothing in here we don't know," Moe said, his voice at a normal volume.

"Nothing?" I asked.

Kristoff shook his head. "Unfortunately, I don't think you'll be able to help."

Bane shifted. "I'm sorry. Is there *anything* we can do?"

Moe answered. "You can tell me whatever it is you're hiding."

I immediately felt a sense of panic set in. It wasn't just my paranoia, after all. If Moe noticed it too, they were definitely keeping secrets.

"What do you mean?" Mary asked.

"There's no way you could know about us and not about anything else."

"I don't know anything else."

"That's impossible," Moe spat. "Your grandmother gave you this book, yet you have no idea where she got it?"

"I believe she wrote it herself."

"It seems so," he answered. "So, where did she get the information?"

Mary glanced at Bane who shrugged.

"I think he's right," I said. "It's time you tell us what you're hiding."

Mary sighed and glanced at Bane again. "Okay, there is one thing."

"But we don't know if it's true," Bane interjected.

"Right. It's not a for sure thing."

I pursed my lips. "Tell us anyway."

"My grandmother, your great-grandmother may have known about your—kind."

"Yeah, we kind of got that," Kristoff said, gesturing to the open book.

"Yes, but she may have known because she was directly involved."

I froze for a split second. "Are you saying she was…"

"No," Mary interrupted. "She wasn't a therian…" she broke off. "She wasn't one of them—you."

"Then what?"

"An ally," Moe said.

Mary nodded. "Yes."

I looked to Moe, waiting for him to elaborate.

"She was one of the allies," he repeated.

"What does that mean?" I asked.

"Back in the early 1900's, before my time, The Order was new. It was established as a way to keep our kind secret. Safe. There were some humans, a select few who knew of our existence and stood with us against the hatred and ignorance rampant in the human population."

"She was one of them?"

Mary nodded. "That's all I know."

"Is it?"

"There is one more thing," Bane said.

All eyes turned to him, and he slouched in his seat. He reached into his pocket and pulled out a slip of paper. "Turn to the last page of the book."

Kristoff furrowed his brow but did as instructed. I watched in confusion as he fingered the jagged edges of a missing page, the one I realized my brother was holding in his hand.

"Bane," Mary whispered.

"It's okay," he said.

"I know you don't trust us," Kristoff said, "but we are not your enemy. Didn't you ever stop to think that you're more like us than you are like them?"

I smiled. "That's something Lucas used to say about me."

Moe nodded. "It's accurate."

Bane inhaled and handed Kristoff the page. We all leaned in for a closer look.

A unique characteristic in certain humans remains the only thing effective to counteract therian curses and magicks. Only one bloodline in human history is known to exist. The link between the mortals and the therianthropes. They are of both worlds and neither.

Although there is much theory and little fact about their origin or if they are still in existence today, there is evidence to support the belief.

"I don't believe it," I murmured. "It's about…"

"Us," Bane said.

I met his eyes. "You knew about this?"

"I couldn't tell you."

"Why?"

He shrugged. "I promised I wouldn't."

I narrowed my eyes. "Again, I ask why?"

He sighed. "Daisy, I met Mary a few years ago and she told me all of this. Granted, I didn't believe it—at least not until I met you and you told me that insane story—but she asked me not to tell anyone and I still felt like I had to keep my word."

I glanced at Mary. "Why did you want that kept a secret?"

"Because of what happened to my mother."

I shot her a puzzled look.

"After your great-grandmother passed away in 1983, she was eighty, the therians came for my mother."

Kristoff and Moe exchanged a look and Bane looked at me.

"What happened?" I asked.

"They killed her," Mary spat. I could see the tears forming in her eyes. "They killed her because she knew too much. I was very young, and another woman took me in. She cared for me, and she hid me. That is, until…"

"Until what?"

"Until she got sick. I watched her wither away slowly."

My heart sank. "Was it…cancer?"

Mary shook her head. "No."

"What was it?"

"Daisy, I know what's happening to Lucas—because it happened to her."

Chapter 33

I HAD *no problem falling asleep. Everything that was going on was enough to knock anyone out. If it didn't keep me up all night, it exhausted me. I couldn't decide which was worse.*

I walked slowly down the street, staring at every house and flowerbed, enjoying the vibrancy. I glanced down to see a familiar gray cat like the one I had seen around my neighborhood. It always seemed to be close for some reason. I smiled.

"Hi, kitty."

The cat meowed and squinted its hazel eyes. I knelt down to pet it and heard a loud, rumbling purr. "You're so friendly."

I stood up to head to the water and the cat meowed at me again. I turned back. "Okay," I crooned, "come on." I gestured for him to follow.

I kept walking with the little striped cat falling into step beside me as if he knew exactly where I was going. I knew I was dreaming at this point, so I wasn't alarmed, I only hoped it wasn't going to be traumatic. At this point, I would not be able to wake myself up. I was too exhausted.

I did know it wasn't just a normal dream. Only the visions were in color. I knew deep down that it meant something and decided not to think about it. I looked down to make sure kitty was still following me. He glanced at me, making eye contact, and squinted at me again.

When I reached the lake, I sat down on the soft grass enjoying the reflection of the sun gleaming off the water's surface. The cat curled up beside me and purred again when I pet him. I half expected to hear a scream for help or a cry of some kind pulling me away from the peaceful scene, but nothing happened. I couldn't decide what the dream could mean if dream boy wasn't even here. Did he send a cat to watch me? I chuckled out loud at the ridiculous thought. At this point, anything seemed possible. I stretched out my legs and leaned back, closing my eyes and enjoying the sunshine on my face. I felt the cat crawl into my lap but I didn't mind. I smiled at him, and he just sat there with his eyes half closed, purring away as if he'd known me for years. I waited for what felt like hours, waiting to either see someone in danger or wake up.

Awaking came first. I looked over at Jess. She opened her eyes.

"Morning," she said with a yawn.

I just stared at her.

"What? Is it my hair?" She reached to the back of her head and huffed.

"No, it's not that. I…"

"You had a dream?"

"Sort of."

"What do you mean sort of?"

I shook my head. "I don't know. It was weird. Weird because it was so normal. You know that cat that's outside sometimes?"

She nodded. "Yeah, it's the neighbor's cat."

"Are you sure?"

She shrugged. "I never thought about it. Why?"

"He was in my dream. He sat with me at the lake."

She pulled her eyebrows together in confusion. "Why?"

"I have no idea."

"Hmm. What happened next?"

"Nothing," I said. "I was just sitting at the water's edge with my cat friend and then I woke up."

"Maybe it doesn't mean anything."

I shook my head. "No. It was in color."

Her face fell. "Oh."

"It felt so real."

"Don't they all?"

I thought about it for a second. "In a way, yes, they all feel real; but this felt…natural. Normal. It felt like a normal day and I just wanted to be alone with my thoughts near the water."

"Hmm," she mused. "Up for a drive?"

I looked at her confused.

"To the lake," she said.

"Really?"

She smiled. "Yeah, why not? I'll bring snacks. If there's nothing there, we can still have a picnic and reminiscence about all the weird shit we shoved in jackasses' lockers."

I burst into laughter. "Oh, Jess, you really are the queen."

"You know it."

I nodded. "Sure. Let's do it."

The drive was mostly quiet, save for the radio that was down so low, it sounded like a hum in the background. We got to the lake and Jess got out, pulling a picnic basket out of the trunk.

"You're such a dweeb," I said.

"Hey, you're the one dreaming about cats and other weird shit. Why can't I bring snacks?"

"Did you have to bring them in a little yellow handbasket like Susie homemaker?"

"Bite me."

"Seriously, though."

"I found it in the pantry, okay? Now hush."

I laughed and sat down on the bank by the water.

"*This was it?*" *Jess asked.*

I nodded. "Exactly, minus the cat."

"Hmm. And dream boy?"

I shook my head. "Not exactly, but I felt sort of…"

"What?"

"I don't know. Sort of like he was there."

She turned to look at me. "You mean the cat?"

I shrugged. "I don't know how, but I feel like dream boy was watching me through the eyes of the cat. It followed me and curled up in my lap and everything. It was really strange."

"At this point, I believe it," she said.

"Really?"

She widened her eyes and nodded. "Hell yeah, Daisy. Crazier things have happened."

I shrugged. "Good point."

"Here," she said, handing me a sandwich.

"Umm…thanks."

"Sure. Now tell me more about the dream."

"There's not much more to tell, Jess. I sat at the lake with a dream cat."

"Only there's no cat here."

I shook my head no and sighed when a heard a tiny meow coming from behind me.

Chapter 34

Nobody spoke for what felt like hours.

"You have to tell us," Kristoff said.

"Who she was?" Mary asked.

Kristoff raised his eyebrows.

Mary sighed then stiffened.

"Please," I coaxed.

She shook her head mechanically. "I can't."

"Who are you protecting?" Moe asked. "She's dead. Who exactly are you so scared for?"

"Myself, okay? I'm scared for myself and my children. They killed my mother! Do you get that? I'm only alive because this amazing woman took me in and hid me away where they couldn't find me."

"They've known about me this whole time," I said. "Lucas wasn't supposed to save me because I'm of that bloodline."

Bane nodded. "Who do you think hit you, Daisy?"

My jaw dropped. "Wait, are you saying the crash…"

He nodded. "Wasn't an accident."

It all made sense now. Everything that happened from the moment that car slammed into mine. I was supposed to die. Mary was right.

"They want us dead," I murmured. "But it doesn't make sense. The Order had me, remember? They let me go because you lobbied for my life."

Kristoff sighed, looking defeated. "Daisy…"

"What?"

"Think about it for a second. The Oder is not what it's supposed to be. Lucas said they were evil, and he's more right than he is wrong. In what world does it make sense for them to just let you go because I said please?"

"What are you implying?"

"I didn't get it before, but I do now. They fear you. All of you. They know you have the power to stop them, even if you don't know how yet. That's why they want you dead. They thought if you knew it was them, you'd retaliate. That's why they tried to crash your car first. Then Lucas came along and screwed up their plan."

"Now, do you understand?" Mary asked. "You're asking me to trust and help the ones who murdered my mother. The ones who want me and my children torn to pieces."

"That's not us!" Kristoff shouted. "It was The Order."

"How can you possibly expect me to trust you when you *are* The Order. You're both members, aren't you?"

"It's not what you think," he answered. "Moe and I are members for no other reason than to know what they are up to, to keep an eye on them. We want to change things just as much as you do, but The Order is a large network and we are only two people. It's going to take time."

Mary shook her head. "I'm sorry, but I can't."

"You don't have a choice," Moe said, rising to his feet.

"What, you're going to threaten me now?"

Moe sighed. "No. We're not The Order, but you do have to tell us what you know."

She set her jaw and growled, "I don't *have* to do anything."

I had to say something. We were getting nowhere. "Mary, I know you're scared, but let me show you something. Follow me." I stood up, signaling her to follow.

She stared at me suspiciously for a moment but eventually stood up. I led her to Lucas's bedroom. He was still lying there, eyes open, completely unresponsive.

"You see him?" I asked. "You see what's happening to him?"

"I can't care about that, Daisy."

"But you *can* care about me. Can't you?"

"I do."

"Then help me," I paused, not trying to hide the pain in my voice. "I love him."

I saw something in her soften. Her face fell and she lowered her head.

"I can't lose him," I said. "If he dies, I might as well be dead, too."

"It's not that I don't care, Daisy. I'm just…"

"Scared," I heard Bane say from behind her.

She turned to meet his eyes. "Yes. I'm scared."

He nodded. "We all are, but that's not a reason to let Lucas die. You can still do the right thing."

"We want to protect you," Kristoff said. He and Moe now stood in the doorway. "We want to make sure whatever you tell us is enough to save my brother. In return, we won't let anyone hurt you."

"But if you don't help us, we can't protect you," Moe advised. "We wouldn't know how."

"Please," I pleaded. "All we need is a name."

Mary sighed, she glanced at each one of us, then took a deep breath. "Her name was Rebekah."

Everyone froze. For a moment I couldn't move. I tried to say something, but I was unable to find my voice.

"Rebekah…" Moe started.

"It can't be *that* Rebekah," Kristoff said. "She was alive in 1903."

"Her daughter wasn't," Mary said.

"Wait…"

"Yes, Daisy. It was a family name. Rebekah and my mother were friends. The Rebekah before her was also an ally. Married to an Errol Black."

"Errol," I echoed. "Lucas was right. He said it may have been Errol who was your relative. Errol was a therianthrope."

Kristoff scoffed. "I really hate that word."

"Sorry. He was one of you. He was a Black. That's how Rebekah knew about you."

Mary nodded. "She passed that knowledge on to her daughter, who was also named Rebekah."

"But I don't understand. You said she got sick—like Lucas."

"She did."

"But I thought this was a therian curse."

"It is. But Daisy, just because therians aren't fully human, doesn't mean they don't share many of the same —components."

"So, this illness can effect humans too?"

She nodded. "None of us are safe."

"Wait," Kristoff said, "the page from that book said something about counteracting curses, right?"

Bane nodded. "A unique characteristic. We've been trying to figure out for a long time what it is."

"Characteristic?" Kristoff said. "Lika an ability?"

Bane shrugged.

"Is there something else you are able to do?"

"Not that we know of."

A realization struck me immediately. "Wait. We know what we *can* do. Lucas isn't technically asleep but…"

"Maybe you can reach him," Kristoff said.

"Yes."

"Do you think he'll know what he needs?"

"I don't know," I answered. "He might; but even if he doesn't, maybe he'll wake up if I can get to him and let him know we're here."

"And if he doesn't?"

"Then we're no worse off than we are now."

Kristoff nodded. "Do it."

"I'll try."

Moe spoke next. "Stay here with Lucas and call me if you need me, but I'm heading to HQ to get this sorted out. Someone knows something about who's doing this."

Kristoff sighed. "Keep me posted. I need answers too, and when I get my hands on them…"

"I know, Son. I'm on it."

I relaxed my body, letting myself fall limp. I focused on the sound of our breath and the beating of our hearts.

I lay still until I felt myself slip into sleep. I reached out in my mind, trying to tether myself to Lucas as I lost consciousness.

"Daisy?"

I opened my eyes and there he was. As real as he'd ever been.

"It worked," I yelled, throwing myself into his arms.

"What's going on?" he asked. "How did I get here?"

I looked around and realized we were in the park.

"Did I do it again?"

"No," I said. "Lucas, we're not really here. You know that, right?"

He looked at me puzzled. "Is this a dream?"

I shrugged. "Sort of. Lucas—you're sick."

"I noticed."

"No, I mean, it's gotten worse. You're at home. In your bed."

He shook his head. "No. I can't be… Am I dying?"

"It's okay. There might be a way to save you. To make you better."

"How?"

"I was hoping you could help me with that."

"Tell me."

"It's a long story and there's a lot to explain, I'll tell you everything—but first, remember that book Mary has? The one that was passed down through her family. It's about us—my family. It talks about my bloodline."

"Yes, I remember."

"It means we can do things that humans aren't generally able to do. It means we're special. What's happening to you is a curse."

"I know that, Daisy; and I know The Order is behind this."

I nodded. "Someone is, but are you sure The Order wants you dead? One hundred percent?"

"Daisy, I stopped telling them about my dreams two years ago and they never even asked me. They don't need me. They *do* want me dead. I promise you."

"You stopped mentioning your dreams?"

He nodded.

"Why didn't you tell me this?"

"I didn't think it was important at the time. Think about it. If I'm in a coma or—catatonic in some way—it's progressing way faster than it did for my mom. No one person has that much power, not even a shifter."

I nodded. "I know. We know whoever is doing this is strong."

"No, it's more than that. My kind are able to harness the energies of the cosmos, it's what makes us capable of shifting in the first place. Some are better at absorbing those energies in the darker hours if you remember Zane."

I shuddered at the sound of his name. "I do."

"But even with those abilities, there are limits. For something of this magnitude, it would take…"

A light clicked on in my brain. "All of them."

"Yes. The entire Order."

"Oh, my god. Lucas, Moe just went down there to try and figure out who's doing this."

"What?" He shouted. "You have to stop him!"

"How?"

"You have to wake up and tell him to stop. They'll kill him, Daisy."

"I can't. I have to talk to you. I have more questions that can help you."

"If you want to help me, save my father. I'm begging you, Daisy, wake up."

"Come with me."

"I promise I'll try but we don't have time for this. *Wake up!*"

I shot up in the bed, gasping. Bane was in the chair across from me. He rushed over. "What happened?"

"Moe," I said. "We have to stop him. The Order is going to kill him!"

Kristoff came rushing into the room. "Did I just hear that right?"

"Call him," I said. "Tell him to stop. I talked to him. I talked to Lucas. I'll fill you in later, just stop your father. The Order is trying to kill you all!"

Chapter 35

KRISTOFF FRANTICALLY CALLED MOE. After three times, he huffed, "He's not picking up. I have to go after him."

"You can't," I argued. "That's what they want. If they're trying to kill Moe and Lucas, getting you to come for them is exactly what they want."

"I know. It doesn't matter, Daisy. He's my father."

I sighed. "I'll stay with Lucas."

Kristoff nodded and headed out to wherever Headquarters was. I stayed by Lucas's bed, holding his hand. His eyes were still open but he hadn't woken up.

"Lucas?" I whispered, my eyes filling with unshed tears. "Lucas, your brother went to find your father and bring him back here. I don't know if you can hear me, but you need to wake up now. You said you'd try to come back with me, so *come back*."

I squeezed into the bed beside him and put my head on his chest, listening to his heartbeat. I wondered if I could reach him the same way I had before, except while awake. I closed my eyes and focused on his scent. Using our telepathic link, I demanded, "Wake up, Lucas," I took a breath and focused harder. "Come back to me. We need you."

I couldn't believe it, but I heard him respond. "Daisy? Is that you?"

I shot up in bed, staring into his still unseeing eyes. "Lucas?"

"What's happening?" He asked, urgently. "Where are you?"

"I'm…wait, where are *you*?"

"I'm still here at the park. I'm guessing I'm still asleep?"

"Yes but—Lucas, I'm not."

"What? So, how are you doing this?"

"I don't know. This has never happened before."

"You really are amazing."

"There's no time for that. You need to wake up. Kristoff went after Moe."

"Meaning?"

"I don't know. I did what you said. I woke up and told him to stop Moe from going after The Order. He tried calling but Moe didn't pick up."

"Oh my god. Daisy, you have to help me wake up."

"How?"

"Just…I don't know. Do something."

"I don't know what to do, Lucas."

"You said you're awake, so you can already do more than you thought. Try to reach through. Try to reach me."

"More than I have already?"

"Yes. Reach with everything you have, every bit of strength you can muster, and pull me out."

"I don't think I can do that."

"You can, Daisy. You're special, remember?"

I sighed, my eyes stinging with the tears I was still fighting. "I have an idea," I said. "Wait one minute."

"Don't break the connection."

"I won't. Well, if I do I know I can get it back, but I can't mess this up."

I left the room and headed back to the kitchen. Mary and Bane were still there, sitting silently as if they didn't know what to do.

"Hey," I said.

Mary looked up. "How is he?"

"Well, you're not going to believe this but…"

"Is he awake?" Bane asked.

"Well no. Not exactly, but he's—here."

They both shot me a lost look.

"You know how I went to him in a dream?"

Bane nodded.

"Well, I somehow managed to do it while awake."

"How?" He asked.

"I don't know but I need your help. Both of you."

"What can we do?" Mary asked.

"Come with me."

They followed me to the bedroom.

I nodded at Lucas. "I can hear him."

"Now?" Mary asked.

I nodded. "I think I can wake him up, but I need your help. Take my hand."

Mary took one and Bane the other, still looking confused.

"Trust me. Close your eyes. Focus on Lucas—hear his breathing, feel his energy. Concentrate hard."

Something rippled through me, almost like an electric shock. I tried not to let it distract me but when their hands tightened their grip on mine, I realized they'd felt it too.

"Lucas?" I whispered.

"I can hear you," he replied.

"How is this possible?" Bane whispered.

"You're all miracles," Lucas breathed.

"We're going to try and pull you out," I said. "You need to push with all your strength."

"I will."

"Reach out with your mind," I said. "See him in your head. Envision him and reach out to him. Pull as hard as you can."

"Daisy, I don't think we can do this," Mary said.

"I *know* we can," I answered. "I feel it. Don't you?"

"I do," Bane said. "Come on, Mom. We can do this."

I almost gasped at the word *mom* but fought the thought away trying to keep my focus on Lucas.

"Now," I ordered.

I envisioned Lucas, beautiful and real in the park with me. I wrapped him in a tight hug. "I love you," I said. "Come with me now."

I pulled away and took both of his hands in mine. I immediately felt resistance, like I was trying to pull him through wet cement.

"Pull," I demanded. "I have him, but you need to help me. *Pull.*"

"Don't let go," Lucas insisted. "I can feel you. All of you."

I blew out the breath I was holding. "Don't break the connection. Use everything you have!"

Another jolt of energy shook through me, this one pulled me out of the grips of my family and back in the real world. I looked at Lucas riddled with guilt. We failed.

"Daisy?"

His open eyes were focused. On me.

"Oh my god. Lucas? Are you here?"

He smiled and I threw myself over the bed and into his arms before he could say another word. His laughter shook through me, lightening the energy in the room.

"I can't believe it," Mary said. "It worked."

"What does this mean?" Bane asked. "Is he cured?"

Lucas shook his head. "I don't think so. If you're feeling a little—off, it's because you lent me some strength. It's temporary. Just long enough to save my family and figure out a more permanent solution. If there is one."

"There is," I assured. "We'll find it."

"I do feel off," Bane murmured. "Tired."

"Don't worry. It won't last long," Lucas said.

"We need to get going," I said.

"We?" Lucas echoed.

"Yes, we," I retorted. "We're not going to argue about this. After what we were just able to do…"

"Fine," Lucas grumbled. "But just you. I mean—no offense—but I can't be worried about them *and* you right now."

I nodded. "Are you okay staying here?" I asked.

Bane and Mary glanced at each other, then nodded.

"I don't feel up for much, anyway," Bane admitted.

"Me, too," Mary answered.

"Okay, call me if you need anything. Lucas and I need to hurry."

I grabbed my jacket off the back of the kitchen chair on my way out the door.

"Damn it," Lucas shouted. "Kristoff took my car."

I looked around panicked. "I'll call Jess."

Lucas crossed his arms. "We don't have time."

"There's no other choice right now."

He huffed but nodded. "Fine."

Jess answered after one ring. "Need me to pick you up?"

"Not exactly," I hedged.

"Oh god, what now?"

"We need your car. It's an emergency, and we don't have even a single second to argue. You can't come with us; and I can't explain why."

"No, I get it. I'm on my way."

She came speeding around the corner in minutes.

"Bane and Mary are inside, so the door should be unlocked. Lock it behind you and *stay put!*"

"Got it."

"Thanks, Jess."

She hurried up the driveway and Lucas peeled out before bothering to make sure she got inside safely. Lucas drove aggressively and I didn't dare ask where we were going. The silence was uncomfortable, but I knew nothing compared to the danger we were walking into. I watched out the window as we passed the Cayucos border.

"Daisy, I know I cannot tell you to stay in the car, but I don't feel I can protect you."

"I know," I said. "You don't have to protect me, Lucas, I feel stronger than I ever have. I feel—different."

"I know that. Your family lent you strength, too. It's why I let you come with me. You're the only one who can possibly break the curse. I know that sounds like something out of a cheesy kid's movie, but you know what I mean."

"I have to admit, I still don't know how."

He nodded. "I know. I'm hoping when you're put in the right situation, it will be instinctual."

"Well, let's hope. We don't have time to figure it out."

Lucas stopped the car at what looked like an outcropping of trees.

"So, The Order are a bunch of elves now?"

Lucas rolled his eyes but didn't bother telling me to be quiet. He pushed through some branches, holding them back for me.

"This is HQ?" I mused.

"No," he answered, pulling back some more foliage from a rockface. "This is."

All I saw was granite and greenery but when Lucas pushed, the rock gave in, revealing an opening.

"That shouldn't have surprised me," I whispered.

Lucas smiled and pressed his finger to his lips telling me to be quiet. He leaned in to whisper. "Stay behind me and, no matter what happens, I want you to bolt if things get bad. Okay?"

He knew me well enough to know I was probably not going to listen, but I nodded since we didn't have the time to argue. We stepped into the room which was basically a cave. It was a very dark, cool hallway with torches on the walls like we were in the 1800's.

I followed behind Lucas until we heard voices. Lucas halted and turned to me. He put one hand up signaling me to stay. I obeyed. I strained to listen as Lucas took a few steps forward. I couldn't make out words. He turned back and waved me forward. We stayed close against the wall. There was a room across the way that didn't resemble a cave at all. There was a beautiful, floral rug that covered the floor and redwood framed furniture, ornate lamps and high-quality upholstered chairs. It looked like a king's old-fashioned bedchamber. I tried not to gasp but was truly amazed.

"Stay close," Lucas whispered. "We have to find Moe."

I followed him past the beautiful room to a larger area that looked less like a living space and a little more like a cave. There was a large wooden table with chairs and what looked like maps and coordinates pinned to the walls. I could still hear indistinct chatter, but the room was empty.

"Where is everyone?" I whispered.

Lucas shrugged and signaled me forward again.

We inched through the main sitting area, still staying close to the wall. It was relatively dark so I wasn't worried about being discovered just yet. We came to another hallway and the muffled voices grew louder and I could finally make out what was being said.

"You should have known better," I heard a man say.

I recognized the second voice as Kristoff's. "So should you."

Lucas stiffened, and I gripped his hand. Staying calm was imperative right now. We couldn't make our presence known until we understood what we were walking into.

"You know everything," the first man said. "We put a curse on your bother because of his betrayal. But his little girlfriend? We didn't count on her surviving that crash, but orchestrating another one would have been too risky. We could have been found out. We thought removing her memories would have been good enough. So, tell me—why wasn't it?"

"I don't know."

A loud crack reverberated through the cave and Kristoff cried out. Lucas stiffened again, fighting the urge to tear someone apart. "You could have killed her two years ago but you didn't. Why is that?" Kristoff asked. "If you're as powerful as you want us all to believe, why is she still alive?"

"You don't know who she is, do you?"

No answer.

"She's of the bloodline. A human with therian power."

"I do know."

"We couldn't just kill her, Mr. Black. You know that. The retaliation—what she and the rest of them could do to us… It could be catastrophic. Don't you understand? This is what The Order was created to protect us from. Our exposure. Our safety."

"What can she possibly do to you?"

"The Order was created to protect us from those people. Most of them were disposed of, but we thought it was over when one daughter went missing. We figured she had been taken care of but, as it turns out, she was taken in by an ally. Someone who we *thought* we could trust. Never trust humans, Mr. Black. She went on to have children and now there are more of them. Enough to challenge us if we don't put an end to them."

"Then why do you need Lucas?"

"We don't," he sneered. "He's a traitor. The orders are to kill him. You and your father unfortunately are just collateral damage. Guilty by association."

"You really think their bloodline could kill us all?"

"Why don't you ask your mother?"

"What the hell does that mean?" Kristoff barked. "My mother is alive. Whatever you bastards did to her, it didn't work."

"Oh, it worked," he answered. "It worked like a charm. Literally. Unfortunately, something went wrong."

"What do you mean?"

"Daisy. That little bitch did something. The crash we orchestrated had unforeseen results."

Kristoff scoffed. "She didn't *do* anything, you know?"

"No, she didn't do anything *intentionally*. None of you are smart enough to figure this one out, so let me simplify it. Triggering her therian powers, her visions created a ripple effect through the universe. We live in a physical world, but the cosmos is more than that. Quantum mechanics are not visual. Outside of the physical presence, probabilities become uncertain. When all possible outcomes are revealed at once, the cloud of probability collapses. She was simply part of a larger chaotic cloud of possible outcomes."

"So, in other words…you have no idea."

I heard what must have been a very aggressive punch. Kristoff groaned.

"I don't expect you to understand, your mind is as feeble as the humans you live among. You and your wicked family. Even your father, an elder… We should have been able to trust *him* at least"

"Where is he?" Kristoff asked. "Where is my father?"

"You'll see him soon enough," he said.

"What the hell does that mean?"

There was no answer. I heard the shuffle of feet, telling me the man had left. Lucas took another step forward, and I followed. I was shocked to see Kristoff chained to a wall by his wrists. His face was bruised and bloody, and his shirt lay in tatters. Slash marks crisscrossed his back. I glanced at Lucas and saw the color drain from his face.

"Why didn't he shift?" I whispered.

"He can't," Lucas answered. "They did the same thing to me. It's like another curse. They chain us up and use a blocking spell to drain our strength. I have to get him out of here. Moe too, but I don't want you to see this. Stay here. Don't move."

I didn't argue but had no intention of obeying, either.

Lucas moved toward a darker corner, and I watched the

shadows twist and morph, trying not to cringe at the crunching and popping sounds I never noticed before. Lucas stalked toward me—as a cat. A small cat, like the one he was when he watched over me from the driveway of my house. How was he going to be able to save Kristoff like that?

I tried to stay put like he said, at least for a minute, but when I heard Kristoff gasp, I took another step. His wrists were free, and he hobbled forward, Lucas the cat in tow.

I wanted to follow but had no idea what was around that dark corner. When I didn't hear screaming, I figured it was safe and followed the boys down the hallway but stayed far enough behind to avoid being seen. We came to another room and Kristoff immediately backed away, pressed against the wall.

The room was full of men and women in dark robes standing in a circle. It was very cliché. I didn't expect The Order to be a stereotypical cult, but I guess I shouldn't have been surprised by *anything* anymore. They were mostly quiet but I could hear soft murmurs. I didn't know what I was supposed to do so I also pressed my back against the wall to be concealed by the dark hallway.

The Lucas-cat crept forward into the room, ears flattened against his head. I held my breath, terrified one would turn around and see him there. Thankfully, they all seemed too focused on whatever it was they were doing to notice. I moved a little closer, making sure I remained hidden, and could see there were smaller rooms attached, almost like small wine cellars. It was dark so I couldn't be sure how far they went back, but I assumed Moe was somewhere in one of them, there just was no possible way to know which one. Lucas seemed to think the same as he entered one. He was completely engulfed in darkness the second he entered the first nook. I chewed on a fingernail, anxiety creeping into my chest, making me feel almost sick as I waited for Lucas to reemerge.

I saw his shape prowling forward, body pressed close to the ground, ears still flattened against his head. He stalked carefully into the next nook and my anxiety intensified. I could hear Kristoff's ragged breathing from a few feet in front of me. I wanted to let him know I was there but didn't want to risk being seen or heard. I glanced up through the shadows and saw there was what appeared to be a wooden scaffold leading up to a second floor. As Lucas crept into the final nook, I made my move. I needed to get up to the second floor and find Moe. He clearly wasn't here. *He must be up there.* I had to be quick so The Order members didn't see me. I had to get by Kristoff, so now was the time to let him know I was here. I only hoped he wouldn't try to stop me. I crept forward trying not to startle him. I whispered his name. He turned, stifling a gasp.

"I'm sorry," I whispered. "I didn't want to scare you, but I had to let you know I was here. I need to get up there," I pointed to the scaffolding.

"Are you crazy?" He hissed. "Daisy, you shouldn't even be here, you're going to get yourself killed."

"Well, can *you* go up there in your condition?"

He closed his eyes and his shoulders sagged. "You know I can't."

"Then hush. I'm doing this."

He opened his mouth to speak, but nodded when I raised my eyebrows. He knew this was the best option. The cross braces were easy to grasp but the wooden planks were splintered or missing. The bars creaked slightly but I moved slowly enough to not be heard. This would not be easy. I used every bit of strength I had to pull myself up, but these weren't like playground monkey bars. My arms already burned, and I had to fight not to let a groan tear its way from my throat. My feet dangled, and I tried to find a foot hold before my arms gave out, but was unsuccessful. I swung my legs forward and discovered a metal bar I could hook my legs around. I kept my hands on the bar above me and bent my knees around the second bar in front of me. I squeezed my leg muscles tight and let go with my hands. I hung there, momentarily upside down before finding another bar to grip onto.

Glad I never had dreams of being a gymnast.

I hurled myself up toward a broken, wooden platform. If I even tried to step onto it, it would creak and crack and I'd be found. I moved to the other side and used another bar to pull myself onto the stone floor of the second story. It was dark and colder than the other rooms. There were no torches or lanterns, but I *knew* something was up here. I just knew it. It would be ideal if we could get Moe and Kristoff out of here without The Order knowing we were ever here. Of course, there was no way it was going to be that easy. I glanced down and saw Lucas in the hallway, back in his human form and staring daggers at me. I knew he wanted to throttle me, but I was shocked when I looked back at him. Lucas was slumped over, looking almost as ragged as his brother. *What was happening?* I knew the answer, of course. The Order. The bastards were gathered here to extend Lucas's curse. I had to find Moe and figure out how to stop them before Lucas lost consciousness again. I had no idea how long his borrowed strength would last. I crawled against the wall to avoid bumping into things as I was completely blinded by the darkness. I felt along the wall until I found an opening and slinked into the room. Here, there were lanterns. It was dim but there was enough light to see exactly what I was looking for. A cell. A stone cage with metal bars like the dungeon of a castle. I stepped closer and could make out a shadow in the cell.

"Moe?" I whispered.

I heard the shuffling of feet as he came to the bars. "Oh, hello, Daisy."

I almost laughed at the formality of his greeting. "I'm here to get you out."

"Yes, I figured that. Are my boys…"

"They're here and they're all right but…"

"But what?"

"They're a little—weak. A little hurt."

Moe sighed. "It's The Order. They're all down there combining their strength to end Lucas once and for all. To end us all."

"We're going to stop them, Moe. I promise. But we need to get you out of here, first."

"Daisy, this place is guarded. They will be coming back. You have to get out. Hide."

I shook my head. "I can't. I'm the only one who can save you now."

"How?"

"Well, we obviously need a key."

Moe scoffed.

"Hey, I'm not suggesting we find one. I'm just thinking out loud. We need to find something to *use* as a key."

"Hair pin?"

I looked at him incredulously. "You watch too many movies. I don't have any pins in my hair."

He huffed. I prepared myself to say something when he hissed my name. I heard footsteps a second later and froze. The guard was coming back.

Chapter 36

THE LIGHT WAS TOO dim but I could make out the silhouette of someone tall, with broad shoulders and strong arms. *I am dead.* I moved back against the wall beside the cell but as he moved closer, I recognized the movement immediately. I knew the way he moved.

"Lucas?"

"Yeah, it's me," he murmured. "Sorry I scared you."

"God, Lucas. You could have said something *before* nearly giving me a heart attack."

"Sorry. I'm here now. And you shouldn't be."

I rolled my eyes.

He didn't say anything, but I knew he wanted to.

"Where's Kristoff?" I asked.

"Stayed behind. We're both a little under the weather."

"They're down there making sure you stay that way," Moe said.

"I know. Let's get you out."

"I'm looking for something to break the lock," I said.

"Don't worry about that. I came prepared." He reached into his pocket and pulled out a little black rectangle.

"What is that?"

"Lock pick," he said. "I almost lost it when I shifted. It fell out of my pocket when I left my clothes in the hallway. I knew we'd be needing it."

I smiled. I should have known.

"Daisy, stand guard."

"Seriously?"

"I'm not asking you to sword fight, just let me know if anyone is coming."

I bit back the sarcasm. "On it."

I listened but all I heard were the soft murmurs of the members down on the lower floor. I could hear the clicking of Lucas's lock pick and the cell door opening made an alarming creak that left us frozen. I waited. It was still silent. We waited a few more seconds and Lucas breathed a sigh of relief and helped Moe wobble out of the cell.

"Are you hurt?" I whispered.

He shook his head. "A little banged up and too weak to shift, but I'll be all right."

I nodded and peeked around the corner, just in time to see who must have been the guard heading down the hallway.

"Lucas," I hissed. "He's coming."

"Damn it," he murmured. He pushed me behind him and readied himself to fight. The guard was big. Bigger than Lucas and definitely stronger with how sick Lucas still was. The borrowed strength was wearing off. I was feeling it too.

The guard approached and halted for a moment when he saw us. His face pinched in annoyance, he grabbed Lucas by the collar of his shirt and hurled him back into the cell against the wall. When he headed straight for me, I ducked, stepping behind him to avoid him. There was no way I could fight him off.

The guard howled in anger and the silence on the lower floor was broken. It was over. We had no choice now but to fight as best as we could. If this was the end, then we'd go down swinging. A ladder was leaned up against the scaffolding, and Order members climbed up at an alarming speed. They'd ditched their ceremonial robes so there was nothing slowing them down. They reached the top floor and barreled toward us. I cowered against the wall, not knowing what I was supposed to do. In the dim light, I saw Lucas's eyes were glowing. So, he was still able to shift. That was good news, but where was Moe?

I heard movement beside me. Panic gripped me until I realized Moe had been there the whole time. At least I knew he was okay, for now. I watched in horror as an array of wildcats, wolves, and foxes brawled in the hallway, some even being thrown to the floor below. I almost covered my ears. I couldn't stand the yelps and howls of animals. Even though I knew what they were, it was hard to hear. *They're not innocent animals. They are bad, evil people. They deserve this.*

The tiger standing beside me *had* to be Lucas. He hadn't moved. He stood in the doorway between them and me. He lunged forward a few times when they came too close but stood his ground. That is, until the other tiger—a white tiger that stood a good foot taller than Lucas—sank his fangs into Lucas's shoulder. Blood leaked from he wound and he let out a guttural growl, taking a swipe at the other cat. As they brawled, there was just enough space between us and the doorway for a smaller animal to get through. Moe and I were both on our feet when a red fox closed the space between us, growling low in its throat and ready to attack. I lunged away just in time, and it followed me out of the nook and into the hallway filled with fighting animals. I dodged as best I could, jumping and ducking, and prayed they were too distracted by who they were fighting to notice me. That hope was in vain. A massive panther perched itself on its hind legs and came down swiping at me.

A burning pain erupted on my chest spreading through me and the slash marks sprayed blood across the room. I screamed but something happened. Everything stopped. The noise, the mayhem. The animals stood frozen as the panther stumbled backwards, trembling and quaking. He was suddenly back in human form, naked, and slumped onto the floor. He lifted his head and glared at me. What the hell just happened?

I tried to withstand the pain, but I couldn't and dropped to my knees. I gripped my chest but couldn't stop the bleeding. I felt someone grab my shoulders and I readied myself to fight through the pain until I heard his voice. "Daisy, look," Kristoff said. "Look!"

I looked up and at least ten of The Order members were human, the rest were running back to the lower floor, fleeing—from what?

"What's happening?"

"You're bleeding."

"I noticed."

"No," he said, stifling a chuckle. "That's what happened. You're bleeding."

I narrowed my eyes.

"That's it," I heard Moe say. "It's your blood. *Your blood is the cure.*"

I was unable to move. The burning in my chest was intense. Lucas took off his shirt, which I clearly didn't mind. He tore it in strips and used them to wrap me in bandages, then lifted me into his arms. My head was foggy, and I was fighting with everything I had to remain conscious. "Stay with me, Daisy."

I closed my eyes. "I don't know if I can."

"Stop being dramatic," Kristoff said. "I stopped the bleeding and you're going to be fine. You're not allowed to die; do you hear me?"

I tried to smile but wasn't sure if I succeeded. "I hear you."

"Good, now we're getting you to a hospital."

"Wait. A hospital?"

"Why not?"

"Well, I don't know. They might have some questions about the jungle cat that tried to kill me."

"Right." He mused. "Humans."

"Besides, we don't have time for that."

"What are you talking about?" Lucas asked.

"My blood. Moe said it was your cure."

"No, Daisy. You're hurt. It can wait."

"Can it?" I pressed.

"Yes," he retorted. "I feel fine."

I snorted, "Liar."

"Okay, fine. I feel terrible, but you're worse off. I promise you, it can wait."

"Take her to Ryly's." Moe suggested.

"Who's Ryly?" I asked.

"A—therian doctor," Moe replied.

I heard Kristoff sigh, but he resisted complaining about his father's use of the word.

They loaded me into the car. Lucas sat in the back seat and made me lie down. I rested my head in his lap, still trying not to pass out. He stroked my hair which, along with the movement of the car, lulled me to sleep.

I didn't dream but I knew this wasn't over. Even as I slept, I was overcome with fear. The Order was still out there. They were everywhere, and I had no idea how my blood alone would be enough to stop them.

I awoke to a familiar beeping noise and opened my eyes. I wasn't in a hospital, but a bedroom. There was an IV in my hand and a heart monitor on my finger. I pulled off the monitor and sat up. Lucas came in immediately. He smiled when he saw I was awake, but he barely looked like himself. His cheeks were sunken in, and his eyes were surrounded in dark circles. He was disheveled and ragged.

"Lucas…"

"I know," he smiled. "I look fantastic."

I frowned, not in the mood to laugh.

"Don't worry about that now. How do you feel?"

I glanced at the IV in my hand. "It doesn't hurt anymore."

"That's the pain meds. You won't be running any marathons for a while."

"Where am I?"

"Ryly's. He's an old friend of Moe's. He's stitched all of us up dozens of times over the years."

"Lucas, you look exhausted. Let me help you."

"Not until you're better."

"I am better. I'm not in pain anymore and I'm not going anywhere. I'm safe here."

He shook his head. "Not yet."

I sighed. "Fine, but don't wait until you're dying again, Lucas. The Order is still out there. Widespread, right?"

He nodded.

"We need you at full strength because this isn't over."

He nodded. "I know, Daisy. But for now, you rest."

Rest sounded nice anyway, so I didn't argue.

Chapter 37

WE SAT in the kitchen trying to figure out how to respond to Moe's request.

"I believe in you," Jess said.

Bane nodded. "So do I."

"We know what you three can do," Moe said. "But the first thing we need to do is heal my boy."

I smiled and held out my arm. Moe reached into his kit to retrieve the needle. "Are you ready?"

I nodded. I winced when he pricked me, but the pain didn't last long. He took about four vials and set them back in the little metal tray.

"That's it?" I asked.

"For now."

I followed him to the living room. Lucas was awake and lying on the couch, but his breathing was ragged and labored. He was hooked up to an IV that was administrating fluids.

"You shouldn't have let it get this bad," I said. "I was fine days ago."

"No, you weren't," he croaked. "Now is fine."

Moe hooked up the IV to a vial of my blood and I watched the color immediately come back to Lucas's cheeks. His eyes brightened and he finally looked like himself.

"That's crazy," I said. "That's all it takes?"

"It's going to take a few more doses over the next few days but he should make a full recovery."

"All this time," Mary uttered, amazed. "I had the power to save…" she broke off.

"Don't do that to yourself," I said. "*None* of us knew. We couldn't have."

She sighed. "I know. It's just hard to accept."

I patted her on the shoulder. "You'll get there."

"We can help, now," Bane said. "We can't change the past but we can change the future. We can stop The Order."

I smiled. "Now that we're back to full strength…with our bloodline, we have enough."

"Enough strength to render The Order powerless," Bane added.

"To keep them weak as mortals with the perfect opportunity for this amazing group of men to reconstruct it and bring it back to its former glory."

Lucas smiled. "It's over," he said. "We're safe now."

About the Author

Sara J Bernhardt is an author and poet who has been writing since a very young age and is a winner of several poetry and short story contests. It is clear that Bernhardt writes in a realistic tone while still creating the enthralling feeling of fantasy. Her writing puts readers in a world that they will truly love to be a part of. Though the writing is edgy and catching it is also not too complex which makes it a comfortable and enjoyable read for everyone.

You can follow Sara at these locations:

Facebook: www.facebook.com/Sara-J-Bernhardt

Also by SARA J. BERNHARDT

https://www.lavishpublishing.com/authors/sara-j-bernhardt/

Summer's Deceit (Hunters Trilogy – Book 1): Jane Callahan is a reclusive, seventeen-year-old high school student dealing with the death of her beloved brother. Her home in Southern California with her mother is a constant reminder of her loss and pain. In hopes of escaping her past she moves to North Bend Oregon to live with her father, where she meets a beautiful boy named Aidan Summers. Jane is intrigued by his looks as well as his unusual ways of attempting to get her attention. After months of uncommon conversation and frustration, an uncertain romance brews between Jane and Aidan, but Aidan has a ghastly secret that could destroy everything.

Summer's Shadow (Hunters Trilogy – Book 2): Aidan Summers, a seventeen-year-old, stunningly beautiful genius, somehow finds his way into the life of Jane Callahan; a lovely girl trapped in soggy North Bend, Oregon. In this new Tale by Sara J. Bernhardt, Aidan relates his side of the story. All of his dark secrets are revealed and all of his motivations behind his strange ways become known as the story unravels in a captivating narrative of suspense, romance, courage...and murder.

Summer's Redemption (Hunters Trilogy – Book 3): The secret alliance of The Silver Wing and the waging war with their evil rival, The Sevren, come into full view in a new light. The evil that still lurks and stirs behind the supposed destruction of The Sevren steps out of the shadows and spins a new tale of adventure, suspense, romance, mystery and terror.

Behind Blue Eyes Series

A father's desire to save his child presents him with an unthinkable choice that leaves him darker than human, forced to roam through time alone as he searches for the place he belongs.

Adam Gold – Book 1: Fleeing the French invasion of Geneva Switzerland in the 1700s, Adam Gold books passage to America with his family. On the ship, Adam's daughter falls fatally ill. A mysterious man comes to Adam with a way to save his child by turning Adam into something darker than human.

The Medallion – Book 2: Adam Gold, an immortal with sweet eyes of blue, rushes through the centuries on a quest for reason and a thirst for revenge. To cope with his pain and regret, he sleeps away the years and awakes in a new era with a powerful, ancient vampire who sets her sights on him.

Golden Shackles – Book 3: When the ancient queen, Sekhmet snatches up Adam, he is faced with a terrifying decision. To help aid her in her vile plans or dare to stand against her.

Plus 3 more segments!

Harvest Moon: Adeline Blackwood is a supernaturally gifted noble young woman who will do whatever is necessary to be with the man she loves.

Also from our Lavish family

Irrevocable Series
Samantha Jacobey
https://books2read.com/IrrevocableSet

The end of the world is coming, or so they say, and that puts Bailey Dewitt on a crash course with Armageddon. Orphaned, she and her young brothers find themselves living with their renegade uncle as part of a group of survivalists. She struggles against them, searching for a way to escape, but every discovery only terrifies her more.

For Caleb Cross, the Ranch is a way of life. The members of their group are family, and none should come between them. Smitten from the moment he met Bailey, his choices are no longer easy, his path no longer clear. He wants to welcome her and the twins into their fold and hopes his kin will agree.

But the elders who lead them aren't interested in the troublesome girl. They are plotting for the time they will be rid of her and expect Caleb to go along with their plans - he is after all one of them.

At first, Bailey resists Caleb's charms, but soon must admit that she desperately needs a friend. She has no intention of anything more, but when the elders make their move, she is forced to trust him with her very life.

They both have hard lessons to learn. Relationships built on secrets and lies don't come with guarantees. When the world falls apart around them, some things are Irrevocable.

The Norn Novellas
A. Nicky Hjort
https://www.lavishpublishing.com/authors/nicky-hjort-1/

The Norn Novellas are all chapters in the epic saga of the youngest and most fickle of the four Norn Sisters. The same feisty immortal creature who must escape her inherent inner darkness to learn the meaning of life.

Each story takes a classic fairytale and spins it on its head, as we learn that maybe Norse Mythology was so much more than legend. And to think, you thought you knew those old tales so well.

Meet Za and find out what really happened...

When Tyndra Turns to Ardnyt - Book 1: In the center of a magical world there grows a beautiful and terrible chasm of climbing plants. On one side of the Ivy Wall we find the hell-of-Tyndra, on the other, the heaven-of-Ardnyt. But legend has it that in the middle...lives a preternatural beast that imprisons and tortures the children from both sides.

When the war against time begins, Azza will have to cross over the Ivy Wall, something that has never been done before by a living being. But if she does make it through, she just might discover who she really is and how she became trapped in this alternate reality.

A fairytale at heart, this is the first chapter in the epic saga of the youngest and most fickle of the four Norn Sisters. The same feisty immortal creature who must escape her inherent inner darkness to learn the meaning of love.

A veritable palindrome from start to finish, the narrative of Where Tyndra Turns to Ardnyt journeys through duality to discover what shocking truths emerge when up becomes down, life becomes death, suffering becomes release, and the most unexpected endings become the most surprising beginnings.

Welcome to a place where forwards and backwards are exactly the same direction. Here Where Tyndra Turns to Ardnyt.

Where Ebon Sounds Like Ivory – book 2: Norse legend has it that the arms of the Yggdrasil tree—a sacred instrument of Odin—are ever-reaching, and its survival is necessary for life itself to continue.

During Winter's Solstice, when the search for her mortal mother begins, Za will have to cross over the Ebon Branch of the Dead—a feat that has supposedly never been survived intact. But if she does make it across and back home, she just might discover why she and the other three Norn Sisters of Fate came to be.

A fairytale at heart, this is the second chapter in the epic saga of the youngest and most fickle of the four Norn Sisters. The same feisty immortal creature who must discover her true origins to understand her inherent inner darkness. Only this way can she learn the meaning of unconditional sacrifice in the name of impenetrable love…when, as her destiny would have it, all the branches of such a powerful tree tremble treacherously in her tiny little hands.

A veritable unraveling of Snow White, the narrative of Where Ebon Sounds Like Ivory journeys through the most horrible of realms where shocking truths emerge. Here where death mimics life, obsession masquerades as devotion, and the most unexpected endings become the most surprising beginnings of a classic tale. One…you thought you knew so well.

Welcome to a place where the darkest of melodies births a miraculous tune of surrenderance. Here Where Ebon Sounds Like Ivory and Christmas, as we know it, begins.

Fairfield Corners Series

L.A. Remenicky

https://books2read.com/FCSet

Small town romance with a paranormal twist! Each in standalone style, read and enjoy any order, any number!

Saving Cassie – Book 1: Some secrets are too dangerous to keep.

After ten years in the big city, Cassie Holt is back in Fairfield Corners. She may look like the same girl who left home a decade before but she's hiding a dark truth from everyone. When her life is threatened by the demons of her past, her best friend—who happens to be the local sheriff—offers his help.

Deputy Logan Miller has been burned by love. He's not looking to get involved but duty calls when the sheriff tasks him with Cassie's protection. Thrown into close quarters with the gorgeous bookseller, sparks fly. Logan is drawn to Cassie, but it's hard to get close to someone who keeps themselves guarded all the time.

To keep Cassie safe, Logan must open his heart but that's something he swore he'd never do.

Ragan's Song – Book 2: One look into his eyes told her she was in trouble – again!

Ragan returned home to celebrate her parent's anniversary hoping they would forgive her the secrets she's kept from them over the last few years. When she discovered that Adam was still living in Fairfield Corners she hoped her secrets were safe, secrets that drove her away three years, secrets that could change both their lives forever.

Adam Bricklin was devastated when Ragan Newlin left town. No note, no email, no text. She was just gone. It has taken three years for Adam to finally move past the heartbreak he suffered when Ragan left town. Now he's moved on and everything was going well until the day Ragan returned to Fairfield Corners. Now the melody that he lost all those years ago is back. It's the same tune he heard that tells him right from wrong—the one that sang Ragan was the one.

Even separation can't silence Adam and Ragan's song, and now that she's back it's time for Adam to decide if he should let the song die or breathe life into it once again.

Where There's Faith – Book 3: A past she can't remember. A love he can't forget.

After losing everything in an accident that he can only blame himself for, Robbie Newlin embraced sobriety and tried to live his life quietly alone at this family's cottage on the lake. Grief being his only ally, Robbie was perfectly content with how he lived until Faith moved into the cottage next door. Now Faith had him questioning whether to keep grieving or to open his broken heart to let love in again.

Faith McMillan had no memory of her life before that day three years ago. The physical scars had faded but the emotional ones were still fresh and raw. Living rent-free seemed like a great way to finish her second book and give her the time to figure out her next move, but then she met the reclusive guy next door and everything changed.

To get past the broken parts, Robbie and Faith must figure out if they want to continue living their lives in solitude or take a chance on finding an ending together.

www.ingramcontent.com/pod-product-compliance
Lightning Source LLC
Chambersburg PA
CBHW070639100726
47907CB00007B/2033